AN A
THE ILLUMINATI CONSPIRACY

F. C. HENDERSON

This book is a work of fiction. As such the story comes from the author's imagination. With the exception of a few publicly known figures and events any resemblance to actual persons is entirely coincidental.

OTHER WORKS BY F.C. HENDERSON:

EARLY RETIREMENT (Murder in Daytona)

SISTERHOOD OF THE SKULL & ROSES

CODY ROSE

THE F-BOMB (Assassination of an American president)

UNEXPLAINABLE THINGS (A Book of Short Stories)

All books are available on amazon.com or
at barnes&noble.com

ISBN # 978-1500450854

2nd Edition

Original copyright June, 2014

all rights reserved

This book is dedicated to all who seek truth

PLAY ME BACKWARDS

I watched them light the candles
I heard them bang the drum
I cried out, *"Mommy I'm cold as ice
and I've got no place to run"*

You don't have to play me backwards
to get the meaning of my verse
You don't have to die and go to hell
to feel the devil's curse

As the night begins there's a pop of skin
then a sudden rush of scarlet
A little boy rides a goat's head
while a little girl plays the harlot

Human sacrifice in an empty church
weep for sweet baby Rose
A man in a mask speaks satanical verse
as he peels off her clothes

I watched them light the candles
I heard them bang the drum

Lyrics by Joan Baez

THE IL-LU-MI-NA-TI

Latin; *illuminatus 'enlightened'* past participle of *illuminare*

a sect of heretics claiming to possess special religious enlightenment or knowledge.

a Bavarian secret society rumored to have been founded by the Fraternal Order of Freemasons

AN AMERICAN IDOL

The Illuminati Conspiracy

PROLOGUE

Jeremy London found fame quickly... Or perhaps it was fame that found him? Less than two years before the dark haired twenty-four year old rock idol was sitting in a claustrophobic ten foot wide by six foot deep cubicle in Cedar Rapids, Iowa taking telephone orders for metric motorcycle parts. The few dollars he earned paid for rent and groceries but it wasn't exactly Jeremy's idea of success. He wanted to be a musician. Now the popular winner of television's 'American Idol' has five chart topping singles and three multi platinum LP's to his credit. He also has over twenty million dollars in the bank.

Billboard Magazine recently dubbed Jeremy London the new king of rock and roll. He's even been invited to lip sync his latest hit record at the upcoming Grammy Awards. The show is being broadcast live from the Staples Center in downtown Los Angeles. The producers want Jeremy to perform the song just before they announce who has been selected as Entertainer of the Year. Those in the know are laying odds Jeremy London will win the Grammy. He had that kind of year.

The singer was supposed to be appearing in his very own prime time pay per view television special tonight. 'Jeremy London Rocks Main Street USA' was to be his first foray into the pay per view market. The show was being broadcast live from Downtown Disney. Of course that isn't going to happen... Not now! The music industry's brightest rising star has been found dead... On Christmas morning no less!

When people first heard the news Jeremy London had killed himself they were stunned. He had become a legacy in the world of rock & roll. His demise is sure to draw comparisons to other musicians who left us before their time. Jim Morrison and Kurt Cobain come to mind, as do John Lennon, Amy Winehouse, Whitney Houston... The list is long.

Questions are sure to be asked. Why would someone as talented and successful as Jeremy London want to die? Why is it the flames of so many young talents are prematurely extinguished? What evil forces cause them to crash and burn before they have a chance to fulfill their destiny?

Please don't get me wrong, nobody is questioning whether Jeremy London's death was a suicide. I mean let's face it, he was found with a rope around his neck. A proverbial smoking gun if there ever was one. Still it is another senseless death in a long line of senseless deaths. They will say something strange is going on in the world of entertainment. So many up and comers expecting to find a pot of gold at the end of their rainbows are instead finding the Grim Reaper waiting there. People are definitely going to want answers... Why Jeremy Tobias London...and why now?

AN AMERICAN IDOL
The Illuminati Conspiracy

CHAPTER ONE

The same question was being asked by every television talk show host and cable news correspondent in the land. It was on the lips of every disc jockey, every record producer, everyone even remotely involved in the rock music industry. Why? Why would Jeremy London commit suicide?

Detective William Durance of the Daytona Beach Police Department wanted to know the answer to that question himself. Spider Will didn't know Jeremy London personally, but he was familiar with the locally born and raised singer's music. Spider was still young enough to appreciate Jeremy's hard pounding guitar licks and strong guttural vocals. He compared London to a young Bon Jovi. The detective doesn't put him up there with Bruce Springsteen though. Not just yet. To Will Durance The Boss was, and as far as he was concerned, always will be, well... The Boss.

Jeremy Tobias London was pegged to be the heir apparent. The next in line so to speak. As such the detective thought the local rock icon's death was worthy of his undivided attention. After all he was the senior officer on duty when the call came in.

Will had volunteered to work Christmas so his married cohorts could be with their families. He was content getting New Year's Eve off. Not that Spider had anyone to celebrate it with. Love had not yet laid claim to his heart. The good news was the man lived in Daytona Beach. He would have plenty of opportunities to fish the Sea of Romance. Daytona Beach beckons bikini clad beauties like a Siren lures young sailors to their deaths. Besides, how much trouble could there possibly be on Christmas morning? Those are the exact words Will spoke when he agreed to work the Christmas holiday. The young detective was about to find out...

The 911 dispatcher who took the call told Will some guy was fishing down by the Main Street Pier when he noticed something swinging between the giant wooden pylons that hold up the thousand foot long structure. The caller said he thought it was a body dangling out there but it was hard to make out in the predawn darkness.

The local yokel who called it in had a holiday tradition of spending Christmas morning fishing down by the iconic pier. He would drive his pickup down to the water's edge, then unload his gear and cast a line. During the busy tourist season he couldn't do that. For one thing he'd have to pay a toll to drive on the beach, and for another he'd have to follow the multitude of superfluous rules imposed by the county parks commission to keep tourist at bay. With the beach toll booths closed for the winter no one was around to enforce any rules today.

After making the call to 911 the guy remembered that he kept a pair of binoculars under the front seat of his pickup truck. He told Will he ran back to get them, then turned and scanned the area between the pylons. Despite the pounding ocean spray and thick fog hovering over the icy cold Atlantic his suspicions were confirmed. An adult male had decided to celebrate the Christmas holiday by slipping a noose around his neck and taking a nosedive off the end of the pier.

There'd be no need for resuscitation efforts. The poor unfortunate was dead long before he was discovered. The moment the police hauled his naked body over the side of the pier they realized identifying the victim wasn't going to be possible without a forensic exam. Because of where the rope had been placed on the man's neck the internal veins in his head had been unable to drain. The result was a vomit inducing, grotesquely bloated purple face. To make matters worse the violent strangulation had caused the guy's eyes to pop out of their sockets. The poor bastards optic globes dangled from his face like giant gobs of snot. Death is never pretty but this one was particularly repugnant.

Detective Durance arrived on the scene just as a local television news crew was pulling in. They'd picked up the call on their police scanner and made a beeline for the pier. It always amazed Spider how quickly reporters could react to a call. It wasn't uncommon for them to beat paramedics to the scene of an emergency. In that brief moment Spider Will flashed back to his soldiering days.

Will Durance had been a corporal in the United States Army. Alpha Company, 3rd Battalion. During his second tour of duty in Iraq Spider's platoon was assigned the dubious task of keeping Iraqi oil fields out of the hands of Saddam Hussein's Republican Guard. Hussein's soldiers were hell bent on destroying the oil wells before the "Devils from America" could steal Iraq's natural resources.

After the events of September 11th George W Bush sent troops into Iraq under the guise they were searching for weapons of mass destruction. His stated goal was to topple the Iraqi government and bring stability to the region. But the president's real goal was to find Saddam Hussein and bring him to justice. George Junior was determined to finish the job his father had started years before with Operation Desert Storm. Securing the oil fields may have played a small part in George W's decision, but it wasn't the main one.

The president's agenda was simple... The solution was not. Nearly five thousand American soldiers were killed in the Iraqi conflict. That number pales in comparison to the two-hundred thousand Iraqi dead. Three quarters of them civilians.

Corporal Will Durance, along with a hundred forty other battle ready soldiers, were given a mission. Secure a remote pumping station used to link the oil fields of Kirkuk with Shurjah Province to the North. According to Army Intelligence insurgents were planning to strike the facility and disrupt the flow of oil to the province's northern borders.

Iraqi success would be strategically minimal, but politically severe, to American interest. Kurdish leaders were already seeking their independence from the transitional government put in place by the allied forces. If citizens couldn't depend on the federal bureaucrats in Baghdad for their security they would look to others for it. The opposition was waiting with open arms...

The American military could not let that happen. Iraqi oil reserves were said to be second only to Saudi Arabia in sheer volume. Saddam Hussein's ruling Ba'ath Party had only tapped the tip of the regions oil producing potential. Studies completed by the U.S. Army Corp of Engineers showed that when it came to the number of active wells pumping crude out of the ground in Kirkuk Province the State of Texas outnumbered them one hundred to one. This despite the fact Kirkuk oil reserves are quadruple what lie beneath the surface of the Lone Star State.

When Will's platoon arrived at the oil fields they found a makeshift elevated train track that ran from the remote facility straight out into the middle of the desert. No one knew why. Soldiers christened it *"The Train to Nowhere."* It was definitely a strange sight to behold.

But not the strangest sight Will encountered during that operation. That distinction belonged to the horde of journalist his platoon found awaiting their arrival at the remote site. Evidently someone in Will's platoon had been overheard boasting about them going on a secret mission. That in itself wouldn't have been so bad had the soldier not revealed the mission's destination. Knowing that, that horde of journalist intended to capture the now not so 'secret' mission on film.

What Will felt when he got to the pier that day was very much the same this time. He thought it macabre that reporters would rush to the scene of a suicide. Besides, what if it wasn't a suicide? Shouldn't the police be able to secure a possible crime scene and gather evidence before the media shows up to televise the event?

Shouldn't a victim's next of kin be notified prior to the public learning their identity? Would they want to learn about the sudden death of their loved ones on the noon edition of the local news?

Not that there was any reason to believe it wasn't a suicide. After all most homicides don't involve a hanging...and there were no signs of a struggle. At least not on the pier. The medical examiner would have to examine the body regardless. A doctor will not sign off on a cause of death if there are questionable circumstances, and in this instance there was.

Ten minutes after Will arrived on the scene the medical examiner showed up. Dr. Clarence Rupert pushed his way through the throng of reporters who'd been relegated to the beach end of the pier and made his way down the wooden planks. With a closed for Christmas seafood restaurant sitting in the middle of the structure he had some privacy to go about his business.

Will expected the medical examiner would perform preliminary postmortem procedures but he didn't. Dr. Rupert took one look at the naked body lying on the wooden pier and announced, *"Suicide."*

It would be hard to argue with the medical examiner's assessment, but the detective intended to just the same. If his mentor had taught him anything it was that, *"Things are not always what they seem."*

Will's mentor, Detective Sergeant Dan Brooks, had been one of the best homicide investigators in the business. Sergeant Brooks came by that distinction in part by not taking things at face value. How often the detective's rule of thumb had proven to be true. If it hadn't been for the final homicide case Detective Dan Brooks investigated before retiring he may have left with a perfect record. That one case haunted him still. Dan Brooks made damn sure his young protege understood he should never take anything for granted.

As paramedics wheeled the unidentified suicide victim to a waiting ambulance Will chased down the medical examiner. He found the doctor standing next to his county owned Ford Taurus sedan filling out paperwork. The detective identified himself then asked the doctor if he would mind answering a couple questions. Without reply, Rupert continued his task. It was obvious he was irritated by the young investigator's interference. Will asked his questions anyway.

"You've been around a while, Doc," he said. *"Tell me, have you ever been called out to a hanging?"* The aging pathologist remained silent so Spider decided to push the envelope. *"How could you determine this was a suicide without even performing an examination, Doctor Rupert?"* Will could see he'd stirred up a hornets nest. The medical examiner put his paperwork down on the hood of his sedan and with finger pointed proceeded to give the cocky young police detective a very descriptive piece of his mind.

"What did you just say to me Detective? Let me ask you a Goddamn question. Who the hell are you to question my expertise? Are you a doctor? I think you better let the professionals determine the cause of death here, Sonny Boy. Why don't you run along now. Go write some failure to flush citations or something..."

The crusty doctor may have thought his outburst would silence the young detective, but it didn't. *"Look, I have a job to do, Doc,"* Will declared. *"It is my responsibility to try to determine if a crime was committed here today. I'm not saying you are wrong, Doc. I'm just asking if you considered the possibility there might have been foul play? Things are not always what they seem, Dr. Rupert!"*

To Will's surprise the medical examiner seemed to consider what he'd said. The look on Rupert's face encouraged him to continue with his diatribe. *"Ain't too many grown men hang themselves, is there, Doc? Especially in the nude like this guy was. I mean, it ain't like he had a lot to brag about... If you get my drift?"*

The medical examiner did. Most men take notice of things like that. Probably much more so than women. It's a guy thing. Many men measure their manhood by comparing themselves physically to their peers. The detective was wrong when he stated not many male suicide victims hang themselves though. Hanging being the number one cause of suicidal deaths among men worldwide. It only ranks fourth in the U.S. however. The doctor wasn't aware of any statistics pertaining to male suicide victims hanging themselves in the nude though. That was something he would need to look up.

Dr. Rupert had been with the county medical examiner's office for the past twenty-two years. The aging pathologist didn't normally go out to crime scenes anymore. His strength was working inside, performing autopsies and analyzing data. These types of calls were for the young bucks on staff. It was where those just starting out cut their teeth, so to speak. Dr. Rupert only responded to this call because like the detective, he was single. With no family or kids to consider he agreed to be on call for the Christmas holiday.

"I'll tell you what, Detective," the doctor offered. *"Follow me out to the morgue and we can find out together. How does that sound?"*

So Spider Will had ruffled his feathers... So what! Whatever it takes. He decided to take the crusty medical examiner up on his offer. *"I appreciate that,"* he replied. *"And just for the record, I think the guy hung himself too, Doc. I just like to be certain."*

Now he'd gone and done it. Spider wasn't the squeamish type but a forensic autopsy would definitely not be pleasant. Not for anybody. Will followed Dr. Rupert back to his office. When he saw the medical examiner pull into a driveway posted OFFICIAL VEHICLES ONLY he pulled his unmarked police car over to the curb and walked around to the back of the building.

Once inside Dr. Rupert handed Will a gown and instructed him to wash up. He was going to give the bullish young detective a lesson in human anatomy. *"First things first,"* Rupert told Will. *"We have to perform a thorough visual examination of the subject and document our findings. Neck markings, groove patterns, skin discoloration, everything. We want to determine that the ligature around the subject's neck when he was discovered is the same ligature that made the marks on his neck. We'll match the rope pattern with the mark patterns on the neck for the same reason. A deep skin test will tell us approximately how long he'd been deceased."*

Will could tell Dr. Rupert knew what he was doing. It comforted him. The crusty old bastard did care after all. He just didn't like having his professional opinion questioned by some dilettante with a badge. Especially in front of other people. As far as Will was concerned that was perfectly understandable. Spider tried to appease him by paying strict attention.

"We will perform a toxicological study to determine if any drugs or alcohol is present in the subject's system." Rupert explained. *"We want to know if there is any possibility he could have been rendered*

unconscious or if he might have had his ability to fend off an attacker compromised."

After his initial exam Dr. Rupert told Will, *"In all probability the cause of death was a combination of Asphyxia and Venous congestion."* He said he based his prognosis on the fact the subject's tongue appeared to be forced up against the posterior wall of his pharynx, blocking the trachea. Rupert explained that with the larynx blocked a person will eventually die of suffocation. In addition the subject's head was engorged. That told the doctor the victim had experienced constricted jugular congestion.

"His death was definitely caused by hanging," Dr. Rupert declared. *"Barring any sign of a struggle I have to conclude it was a suicide. We will of course run more tests."* The medical examiner showed he had a sense of humor when he added, *"After all, things are not always what they seem... Isn't that right, Detective?"*

Will couldn't argue with the medical examiner's findings, and that was okay. He'd assumed all along the death was a suicide. He just wanted to be sure. This was not his first rodeo. The detective had been called out to investigate plenty of suicides. The last one had been a shotgun blast to the face. Spider wasn't sure what was worse, someone blowing their head off with a shotgun or what he'd witnessed today. At least with a shotgun it was over and done with. This poor bastard had been hanging off the end of that pier for quite a while. Death must have taken several minutes at least. Several eye socket popping, tongue tearing, excruciating minutes.

The medical examiner removed his surgical mask then looked at Will and said, *"Sucks to be him, Detective."* There was still the matter of identifying the deceased. Once Will knew who he was he could notify the next of kin, if there were any. He knew many of these type of cases end up in Potter's Field. For those poor souls no one ever comes forth to claim the body. It's quite sad... A life not lived.

AN AMERICAN IDOL
The Illuminati Conspiracy
CHAPTER TWO

Jeremy London was raised in New Smyrna Beach, Florida. His dad sells insurance there. His mother is an elementary school teacher. Neither parent spent much 'quality' time with their son when he was growing up. Once he reached puberty Jeremy was relegated to the bottom rung of the importance ladder so to speak. Replaced in his parents eyes by careers that could not love back and other assorted interests that left his parents unfulfilled.

Larry London's real passions were playing golf and target shooting. Most weekends he could be found playing a round of eighteen somewhere. Either that or at the shooting range. Both pastimes are something Larry was good at. Besides, they provided him a way to connect with his business clients.

June London teaches fourth grade. Her evenings are usually spent grading papers and pouring over student assignments. When not doing that she can be found studying her bible. June is a very good teacher. Her students adore her. Jeremy on the other hand always found his mother to be rather condescending. Detached from reality by her religion.

June and Jeremy's biggest disconnect was her insistence that he be born again. June sees her faith as life giving truth while Jeremy views it as a means of escape. As far as he was concerned people flock to God to evade their responsibilities. Case in point... Whenever Jeremy would ask his mother for something her response was always, "I'll talk to God about it."

June had been browbeating her son to accept Christ as his personal savior for years. She accepted the fact her husband was lost but she desperately wanted Jeremy to get saved. Baptized in the blood so to speak. She tried to help the Holy Spirit along by prodding him at every opportunity.

Somehow it almost worked... Almost. Each Spring June London's Pentecostal Church holds a revival service on the beach. The entire congregation meets at the beach and reaches out to the unsaved who happen by. They see it as their Christian mission. June connived her son into attending.

Unfortunately the event didn't go so well. When June's pastor, a passionate man with a fervent desire to do God's will, made a plea for those in need of prayer to come forward Jeremy stood. It was a moment he would come to regret.

After receiving a laying on of hands Jeremy took the proverbial leap of faith. He repeated the words the pastor prayed, asking God for forgiveness and for the Holy Spirit to come into his heart. Eight other converts stepped forward to commit their lives to Christ that day too. The church's Pentecostal doctrine required new converts to publicly acknowledge their commitment to God by being baptized. Jeremy, being the youngest, was chosen to go first. He'd recently turned fifteen.

The perpetually exuberant pastor led the teenager into the cool Atlantic surf as his worship team was finishing their song of praise. Then he began the ritual. He was about to address the congregation when he was interrupted by a throng of unruly teenagers who'd been hanging out on the beach watching. They were shouting derogatory comments. Most directed at Jeremy.

Jeremy recognized them. The misbehaving throng of delinquents went to his school. Some of them were pointing at him and laughing. "Did Jeremy go to church with mommy this morning," one of them hollered. "No more going down on your boyfriend" yelled another. One kid Jeremy recognized as being on the high school football team pulled out his dick and hollered, "Hey, London... As long as you're on your knees!"

Red faced and embarrassed, Jeremy bolted. Being fifteen he didn't realize running away would only seal his fate. The worst was yet to come. These bullies could be brutal.

June London was beside herself with anger. She'd waited a long time to witness her son's baptism. She told everyone around her the young convert was her Jeremy, and now she had to eat humble pie. Amazingly her anger wasn't directed at the hoodlums shouting the blasphemous slurs. It was targeted at her son.

Jeremy never went back to church after that. He would rather go to hell than have to deal with that situation again. His relationship with his mother continued to deteriorate. June never forgave him for embarrassing her in front of all her church friends.

With very little family contact and few close friends Jeremy needed something to occupy his time. He bought himself a guitar. It wasn't fancy but it was his. The kid saved most of the summer to afford it.

The black on black Epiphone model six string came with glowing recommendations. The instrument was well made considering its one hundred dollar price tag, which included a small amplifier. The first thing Jeremy did was replace the guitar's stock strings with medium gauge polyweb ones, then he set out to learn how to play. Before too long the teenager was strumming out Led Zeppelin tunes. Jimmy Page, Led Zeppelin's iconic lead guitarist, became Jeremy's idol. He patterned his style and his look after the English rock star, who happened to be something of a child prodigy himself. After Jeremy changed his look and learned to play the guitar many of the girls in school thought he was cool. His long dark hair, which he purposely styled to resemble his idol's, attracted them like bees to honey. The self taught musician took advantage of it. When his mom was at church and his dad was on the golf course Jeremy usually invited some starry eyed teenage debutante up to his bedroom.

When he finished high school Jeremy ran off and joined a rock band that traveled the regional circuit. They called themselves SHARK BAIT. The group was based in Daytona Beach but played all over the southeastern United States. Jeremy saw an ad for a lead guitarist the band had placed in a local newspaper and tried out. The other members of the band were a bit older than him but that didn't seem to matter. His talent was evident to all who heard him play.

A year or so after Jeremy joined the band they split up when two of the band's founding members got busted in a drug raid. Dejected, Jeremy returned to New Smyrna Beach intent on pursuing a music career. The area was loaded with venues where he could find gigs and hone his craft. They just didn't pay much, if anything. Jeremy would spend an hour loading up his gear and driving to a gig, then play a three hour set before driving an hour home. For his efforts he might earn a hundred bucks.

It didn't take long for him to realize he couldn't survive on his music alone. Good guitarist or not Jeremy was going to have to get a job. He heard a metric motorcycle parts distributor up in Flagler County was hiring so he grabbed his guitar and headed up the road.

Jeremy had some knowledge of metric motorbikes having owned a Honda Shadow. What he didn't know he'd learn. The job paid fifteen bucks an hour. Over the course of a week that was a lot more than he could earn playing Zeppelin covers.

A year or so later the economy bit the dust. Nobody it seemed was buying motorcycles or the parts they needed to keep them running. The parts distributorship had to cut its workforce by twenty percent. Jeremy got lucky. When the owner first heard that one of his newer employees was a professional musician he hired him to entertain the troops at the company Christmas party. Like most people who heard Jeremy play for the first time he was impressed. Jeremy would not be laid off, but he would be required to transfer to another site if he wanted to keep his job.

Company headquarters were in Cedar Rapids, Iowa. That's where Jonathan Heller, president and founder of Hell on Wheels Motorcycle Parts Incorporated grew up. Heller started the business working out of his parent's basement. Ten years later he was a multimillionaire. Wanting to keep his musically talented employee close by his side he offered him a job in Cedar Rapids.

Jeremy spent his twenty-first birthday on the phone selling Honda parts to some kid in California. His boss gave him a raise when he agreed to make the move so Jeremy was now pulling in over seven hundred bucks a week. His work schedule precluded him from taking gigs though. The only work Jeremy got was the occasional company party. That and the annual Battle of the Bands competition held in neighboring Davenport.

In the spring news came out that the American Idol television show was going to hold open tryouts in Des Moines. The program was a national sensation. It had held the top spot in the Neilson rankings for eight years running, but beginning with the upcoming season the show was going to have competition. Copycats like The Voice and X Factor were going after its viewers. The show's producers were determined to find the talent they needed to keep their show number one.

After watching Jeremy win the Battle of the Bands competition over in Davenport that winter Jon Heller insisted his young employee try out for American Idol. He even had his chauffeur drive him to Des Moines. Jon Heller not only believed his guitar playing employee would make it through the initial audition. He believed he'd make it all the way to the live rounds in Hollywood.

The metric motorcycle parts magnate wanted to be around when that happened. If his employee was the real deal Jonathan Heller intended to ride the kids coattails all the way to the top of the charts. What better marriage was there than rock and roll and motorcycles?

It didn't hurt that the self made multimillionaire knew rock icon and

American Idol judge Stefan Tayler personally. It just so happens Tayler owns a collection of vintage motorcycles that would make Orange County Choppers jealous. In fact the rock star's T-4 Hotrod was the concept bike for Honda's Valkyrie Rune. It is a world class collectors item.

Just two years before Heller had offered Tayler two hundred grand for the bike. He was hoping to make it the centerpiece of the motorcycle museum he was opening just outside Cedar Rapids. Tayler insisted he wasn't selling. He did however donate a vintage motorcycle to Jon Heller's museum collection. A 1974 BMW Motogrotto cafe racer.

American Idol has been the catalyst of several musical superstars. The shows producers aren't shy about advertising that Idol alumni have achieved nearly four hundred number one records since the show's inception, or that singers who've appeared on Idol have sold over sixty-million albums, making dozens of them wealthy beyond their wildest dreams.

The good news for Jeremy was that the shows last five winners have all been white pop singers who played guitar. It seems his genre has been well represented. With a little luck and determination Jeremy intended to make it six.

Auditions for the show were being held at The Temple Theatre. The former Masonic Lodge had been converted into a performing arts center in downtown Des Moines. Jeremy arrived in plenty of time to meet Idol judge Stefan Tayler, who'd come backstage to greet him.

The singer told Jeremy he had heard a tape of him doing Dazed and Confused and was very impressed. The Zeppelin song was one of the rocker's favorites. He told Jeremy there would be no favoritism shown, but that he was confident he would do just fine. Tayler's only advice was, "Stay Cool!"

Well over nine hundred wannabe recording artists showed up for the audition. Jeremy was the fifteenth to be called to the stage. He did a sweet rendition of Zeppelin's Dazed and Confused, which earned him the right to come back later in the day to perform a second number. He chose another Zeppelin song, 'Going to California.'

The Jimmy Page composition ended up being the perfect song choice. It gave Jeremy the opportunity to showcase his voice as well as his guitar playing. At the end of the day Jeremy London was one of eleven chosen to continue their adventure in Hollywood.

Long story short, Jeremy made it to the final round of American Idol. With Stefan Tayler providing the impetus Idol judges bestowed the singer with praise. Seems viewers followed their lead because on the final night of competition Jeremy London was crowned the winner of American Idol.

A guaranteed recording contract would provide Jeremy with riches beyond his imagination. His first single, released by media giant Head-Hunter Records, shot up the charts. It reached number one in just two weeks. By month's end the Jeremy London composition went multi-platinum. The song's title, 'Hell on Wheels,' was ironically the name of his previous employer's motorcycle parts company. The song is about a young race car driver who sells his soul to the devil in return for stardom on the racing circuit. The last two stanzas read like this;

You were first to cross the finish line
Pledge allegiance to the checkered flag
There is no turning back from here
Lest it be in a zippered bag

Win, you lose... Lose, you win
The story ends the same
You wanted to be Hell on Wheels
For the glory and the fame

Hell on Wheels, Hell on Wheels
Went to Hell... To see how it feels

No turning back, There is no road home
You have gone to Hell on Wheels

A second number one hit soon followed. Then another. By year's end Jeremy London had amassed a pretty sizable fortune.

Following the massive success of his first LP Jeremy was approached by high level executives from his record company. They showed up at his house to make him an offer he should not refuse...

He was told the world would be his for the taking. Head-Hunter Records would guarantee Jeremy continued success. Movie deals would be made. Millions of dollars in advertising money would be his. He'd be on the cover of every magazine in the country. He would appear on every television network in the land. Jeremy

London's face would be more recognizable than Jesus Christ. And in return all they wanted was his signature. It was a stunning concept. One that didn't really seem real.

Jeremy had met a girl a few months before this offer came in. Her name was Felecia. She was a sound engineer at the studio where Jeremy was working on a track. After a couple dates Jeremy had asked her to move in with him. He really wished she was there now. He wanted to talk to her about it. The girl had a way of putting things in perspective. Unfortunately she'd gone to San Francisco to visit a friend for the weekend. When the CEO of Head-Hunter Records pulled out a prewritten contract for Jeremy to sign the young rock star didn't even blink. After all, what was good for him was good for them. If he made money, they made money. Right?

Elliot Prince was the CEO of Head-Hunter Records. When he drove out too Malibu to visit his new rock star he didn't come alone. In tow was Shep Dellas, the lead singer of British rock group, STONE BLIND. Shep The band had won that year's Grammy award for Best Male Rock Act. They were joined by the female rock duo, PINK RIOT. Telisha Barr and Mindy Cypress had collaborated with STONE BLIND on the top selling record of the previous year, a CD titled 'INCARNATE.'

The two were hot as burning embers. Telisha was Latino. She had a pair of caramel colored double D's that defied the rules of gravity. Mindy on the other hand was kinda small on top. But she had a behind that belonged on a food platter. Neither of them was shy. Needless to say the rest of the night consisted of a combination of sex, drugs, and rock and roll. Jeremy couldn't believe he was snorting cocaine through rolled up hundred dollar bills pulled from the wallet of the CEO of his record company. By mid morning the next day Elliot Prince had Jeremy London's autograph. The singer was now signed, sealed, and delivered.

But to whom? What exactly had he signed? Jeremy figured things would continue as they had. He'd play his guitar and sing his songs, and the money would continue to roll in… And it did. Only this time with conditions. It was all there, written in the fine print…

Jeremy would no longer be choosing his own music. He'd sing what he was told to sing. It wasn't that the songs he was given weren't good. In many ways they were better than his. Technically the music was dead on. It's just that he would miss the emotional connection. When a writer puts pen to paper the ink on the page might as well be his own blood. His lyrics express who he is as a person.

Most of the songs Jeremy had recorded up to then were very contemplative in nature. People could identify with the situations he wrote about. He was in large part a spokesman for those without a voice. The material he was being given now lacked that. The lyrics were lost in the driving beat of the music. Jeremy London's new songs became universally desired, while simultaneously forgettable.

Several of them made reference to the world becoming one, and not like John Lennon's *Imagine* had. John had asked his listeners to simply consider there might be a better way. He reminded us of our universal similarities, and suggested alternatives to the way things were done. The lyrics Jeremy was given spoke of world domination. A world led by greed. A world where the population was controlled, and thinned, to make room for those who "belonged."

Other songs elicited Orwellian ideas of a world to come. One song, 'Paperless Society,' spoke of a monetary system that exists only in cyberspace. To play and pay one would need to have 'the code.' Having the code would allow a citizen to live in harmony with his fellow man. The catch was you didn't decide if you had the code... They did!

Then there was the lyrics to Jeremy's latest number one hit record, 'Celluloid.' The song had a rocking beat people found intoxicating, and a guitar solo that was sexually exciting...but oh, those lyrics!

> *"Hear me out, you who know*
> *That I come not from form but from void*
> *Please understand... I am your friend*
> *The all seeing eye... Celluloid"*

> *"I was there in the beginning*
> *I'll be there when it ends*
> *Will you be with me, my friend*
> *Only those with the code can determine Who, What...and When*
> *You don't? I'm so sorry...*
> *Guess we can't be together... You're not... Celluloid"*

The song went number one almost overnight. iTunes recorded over one million downloads within hours of its release. That caught the attention of Super Bowl sponsors, who wanted Jeremy to perform the number during the game's half time show. There was no bigger stage than the Super Bowl. One hundred and fifty-million viewers were expected to watch the game on television.

Like most Super Bowls, a huge production was planned. The scenario had Jeremy dressed as a futuristic space traveler arriving in the stadium on a Star Trek like star ship. A cast of one thousand similarly dressed earthlings appear from the shadows and bow to him in reverence. A low hum builds through the stadium as the space traveler is slowly enveloped in a swirling bright light. Once he is completely bathed in light it suddenly goes out.

Simultaneously the low humming noise that had been building since Jeremy first arrived will have reached an ear shattering crescendo. It too will stop suddenly, conjunctively leaving the stage in an eerie, pitch dark silence. After several crowd confusing seconds a spotlight will illuminate Jeremy yet again.

The audience will find the singer has levitated off the stage and is now hovering high above the thousand plus cast members below him. They have their hands raised to him in praise. Jeremy, as the space traveler, begins to separate the huddled mass of worshipers into two groups. It will be obvious to the television audience that being chosen for one group is much preferred over being relegated to the other. Much like the Gestapo did to the Jews when they disembarked the cattle cars in Auschwitz.

With the two groups separated Jeremy floats back to his star ship, which we discover has transformed itself into some sort of futuristic throne. As he approaches his throne a mysterious, well developed, two headed woman appears out of the darkness. She's been made to resemble some sort of long curvaceous lizard. One of her heads appears to be in a state of euphoria while the other transcends deep sorrow. In her hands she carries a large jewel encrusted crown. At the center of the crown a Rams head has been imbedded, its long curled horns point upward.

The sexy dual headed behemoth bows to the rock star then places the over-aggrandized crown on Jeremy's head. At the same time the now familiar hum begins to swell in full stereophonic glory. The newly crowned Space King stands as his worshipers bow in unison. What happens next stuns the crowd. Jeremy waves his right hand over his followers and half of them fall dead.

His remaining followers begin to celebrate what they perceive was a living sacrifice. Then Jeremy lifts his other arm. As he does the humming again builds until it reaches a crescendo. Suddenly there is a brilliant flash of light. The Super Bowl audience looks on as the remaining earthlings assembled on the football field fall dead too. Simultaneous to what is happening on the field a shower of glittering neon dollar bills is being blown throughout the stadium, helped along by giant wind turbines built especially for the occasion. Neon colored money rains down on the crowd like confetti from heaven.

The half time show culminates with Jeremy London, aka the Space King, going into a raucous rendition of his smash hit, Celluloid. As he rocks the Super Bowl giant screens on either end of the stadium show football fans climbing over one another in a frenzied attempt to accumulate the glittery cash raining down around them.

Five weeks later it all comes too fruition. Despite a rash of complaints from some viewers Jeremy London's fame grows. Of the nearly two hundred million people who watched the Super Bowl half time show only a small handful caught the bevy of subliminal messages that producers had interspersed throughout the production. The most obvious being the almost indecipherable chant the cast moaned before they all ceremoniously died. "Novus... Ordo...Seclorum. Novus…Ordo…Seclorum. The Bright and Morning Star."

Surreptitiously placed cryptic messages flashed across television screens in millisecond bursts too. Images of ancient gods like Belial, Belaphor, and Molech, all made an appearance. These images were interspersed with a rotation of swift moving milli-bursts depicting ancient symbolism. Viewers were subliminally subjected to Swastikas (an ancient symbol representing the changing of seasons), The number 666 (presented in a three lined synchronized circular labyrinth), and an Udjat (a reptilian eye encapsulated in a pyramid, a Masonic symbol seen on the backside of the American one dollar bill).

Viewers were also subjected to a burst of rapidly alternating images of what's come to be known universally as a peace sign. What a misnomer that one is. A broken inverted cross incarcerated in a circle, (the circle itself symbolizing eternal and everlasting). Anton Lavey used that very same symbol as the backdrop for his alter when he founded The Church of Satan.

Meanwhile back in New Smyrna Beach, Florida Jeremy London's Super Bowl performance was being closely monitored by his born again mother. His Pentecostal Christian born again mother. The ghoulish images had not escaped her watchful eye. June London's son had made the ultimate sacrifice. He had sold his soul to the devil. She was convinced of it. She could see it in his eyes. June London spent the rest of the night on her knees praying for her only son's deliverance.

AN AMERICAN IDOL
The Illuminati Conspiracy

CHAPTER THREE

The Illuminati had its genesis in the year 1776. Membership in the ultra secret society came from within the upper hierarchy of the Fraternal Order of Freemasons, who were themselves a somewhat secretive organization. They had sprung up earlier that century. A few of their members had been associated with a pre Freemason organization known as The Enlightenment. This was a group of free thinkers who were deeply opposed to both government intervention and the Catholic Church.

Throughout the eighteenth century the balance of power in Europe was firmly in the hands of the few. Those in positions of authority believed groups like The Enlightenment were dangerous. These so called intellectuals could cause some commoners to question their Lordships and wreak havoc on public opinion.

Thus began a campaign of propaganda aimed at misleading the minions. Books were published claiming dangerous groups like The Enlightenment was conspiring to bring down the Catholic Church. It was said the men who belonged to this group were diabolically opposed to Christ. Some even went so far as to claim the free thinking intellectuals who were said to make up The Enlightenment were traitorous mystics, and that they were responsible for starting the French Revolution.

Several of these propaganda publications became quite popular. With conservative politicians and powerful orators of the church providing the impetus members of The Enlightenment were vilified. Sweeping new laws were passed outlawing membership in such groups. Power to the people was a concept that needed to be squashed. With no chance of ever becoming mainstream, and the threat of arrest hounding them, The Enlightenment dispersed.

Learned men who believed that the expression of human thought and the right to question the church was providential needed a platform from which they could vent. As intellectuals they believed it was their responsibility to promote the advancement of science and rid the world of superstition. These men regarded as fools those who deftly followed the Vatican's interpretation of God's great plan for mankind. They began organizing into secret societies.

These secret societies were able to grow their membership by appealing to hardcore constituents with similar beliefs. Like the men who once made up The Enlightenment these men also believed in individual empowerment, and fought against the authority of State rule. They saw the Catholic Church's domination over philosophy and science as an abuse of power. They were among the first to seek intellectual equality for women, and support efforts to improve educational opportunities for those who desired it. As time went on some of these secret societies flourished. One of the largest and most influential being the OTO.

Ordo Templi Orientes (OTO) was founded in the early 1900s. Like the Illuminati they too were a secret suborder of The Freemasons. The quasi religious order was said to have enrolled thousands of members. Its best known was an occultist named Aleister Crowley.

Mr. Crowley wrote what would become known as the Ordo Templi Orientes 'Book of the Law.' That book laid down the tenets the order would follow to this day. It was for all intents a book of philosophical law. Its pretense was that one should follow their own will in life. It was up to every individual to determine who they were created to be, and what they were created to do. Even why they were created at all. Once a person's 'true' will was revealed that person could reconcile his destiny.

To quote Crowley, "One must find out for oneself, and make sure beyond doubt, who one is...what one is...and why one is. Being thus conscious of the proper course to pursue the next thing is to understand the conditions necessary to follow it out. After that one must eliminate from oneself any element alien or hostile to success. One must develop those parts of himself which are specially needed to control the aforesaid conditions."

Aleister Crowley contributed yet another equally important doctrine to the Ordo Templi Orientes. He wrote the secret order's 'Gnostic Mass.' Crowley's Gnostic Mass replaced accepted Christian tenets of faith with the occultists own warped principles.

The master manipulator and self professed orator created a rite of ceremony in which a female deacon (High Priestess) takes 'The Book of Law' (Aleister Crowley's so called Bible) and leads those gathered in repeating the 'Gnostic Creed' (yet another Crowley invention). OTO members then announce their belief in their Lord, the Sun, the Air, Baphomet, and the Gnostic Church.

Once that is done they take part in the Eucharist, were they confess their rebirth as incarnate beings. Once everyone has partaken of wine and cake the female deacon entreats Baphomet, the sabbatic goat deity, by making the following declaration.

"O Lion, O Serpent, be mighty among us. Do what thou wilt. Be the whole of the law. The Lord blesses you, the Lord enlightens you, the Lord brings you to accomplish your true will. Yours is true wisdom, and perfect happiness."

Insanity? Perhaps...but thousands believed.

As for the Illuminati, actual membership numbers aren't known. Fact is the society's actual existence is in question. Many believe the Illuminati is a figment of overactive imaginations. The idea that a small group of individuals could control world events and actually manipulate entire societies of people is simply...not possible.

They blame conspiracy theorist, who claim the Illuminati is made up of notable people, all hellbent on creating a one world government. These theorist contend that American Presidents, corporate leaders, Hollywood executives, and their counterparts worldwide are all in cahoots to tear down the falseness of the Christian Church and other superstitious entities invented by man to keep free thought at bay.

But the simple truth is the Illuminati does exist. It is in essence a society within a society. The Fraternal Order of Freemasons has played a role in creating the fabric of our country since before the American Revolution. Early in our history Freemason membership in America included George Washington, Benjamin Franklin, Paul Revere, Andrew Jackson, and many others. It has been suggested that Freemasons were responsible for the Boston Tea Party, as well as other acts of terrorism against English royalty. Some of these men were in fact, Illuminati.

Christian religious organizations have objected to the existence of Freemasonry from its very inception. The organization's most vocal opponent has been the Roman Catholic Church. In 1917 the church's Code of Canon Law was changed to specifically declare any catholic found to be a member of the Freemasons automatically excommunicated from the church.

Because the Fraternal Order of Freemasons appears to have become more mainstream in recent years the Catholic Church has backed off somewhat. Membership in the Freemasons, at least at the local level, now tends to be of a social nature. Members come together to celebrate their brotherhood and be a service to their communities. The church's code still exists but it is rarely used because church leaders believe the Freemasons true calling has been relegated to the back burner.

Free thinkers. Men of vision. Enlightened men who understand that for the world to survive, and for man to fulfill his true destiny, he has to comply with the natural order of things. The Illuminati is dedicated to mankind becoming one with his destiny. It is an organization dedicated to the idea of a one world government. A world where man is free to develop his idiosyncratic self. Illuminati have infiltrated every conceivable crevice of corporate business and high finance. Every possible place where the deceived can further their cause by poisoning the environment they dwell in.

Illuminati exist in the highest reaches of government. They reside in the highest offices in the land. They control the content of our very lives. From the movies we watch, to the music we listen to. From the products we buy, to the medicines we ingest. They decide who reigns and who falls. Who reaches it to the top of their chosen professions and how long they stay there. They determine who lives...and who dies!

Jeremy London was sitting on top of the entertainment worlds dung heap. He was revered, almost lionized, by hordes of music fans. He'd earned millions of dollars, with many more promised. He was King of the Mountain. Jeremy London was The American Idol.

But to remain there he needed to comply. He had made a pact with them, and it was sealed in blood. Jeremy London made his bed and now he had to lie in it. Perhaps he was deceived. Maybe he didn't understand what he was getting himself into. It's possible he was blinded by all that sex, and money, and drugs... Hey, that's rock and roll!

Did they need him? You bet they did. To get their message out they needed to reach people. It was determined long ago the best way to accomplish that was subliminally. Most people are mentally lazy. It's been scientifically proven that on average human beings use only ten percent of their brain capacity. People get by putting out as little effort as possible. Sweat equity is a concept we lost centuries ago. Instant gratification is the word of the day. Modern man wants it, and he wants it now. Leading people where you need them to go is as simple as dropping a rope from heaven. Lead a sheep to water and the rest will follow like calves to the slaughter.

The Illuminati know how the game is played. They understand some sheep comply and some didn't. Those that do enjoy long very successful careers. They earn fortunes far beyond their ability to spend them. It's true they sold their souls in the process, but that is the cost of doing business.

There used to be this television commercial aimed towards people who fail to maintain their cars properly. Its catchphrase was *"You can pay me now, or you can pay me later."* Bottom line is... Everybody's gonna pay!

Jeremy London was drowning. He just didn't know it. The popular rock star was cruising around in an ocean of money but his boat had a hole in it. Maybe if he'd stayed and gotten baptized that day? If he hadn't run like a scared kitten when those kids on the beach messed with him. Maybe?

Nah... Religion is just man's way of self controlling his excessively bad behavior. Otherwise we'd have killed one another off centuries ago. Believing in God is like believing in the Easter Bunny or Santa Claus, is it not? We're all here because the planets lined up in just the right sequence one day. The circumstances were just right. It was a one in a billion chance. Nature mated with fate and here we are. God doesn't exist...but don't tell that to Jeremy London's mom. Because she is on her knees praying to Him for her son's soul...

AN AMERICAN IDOL
The Illuminati Conspiracy

CHAPTER FOUR

Like many corporate power mongers Elliot Prince is both money hungry and egotistical. But the CEO of Head-Hunter Media Group is more than that. He's also a shameless sexual psychopath who'd sell his mother to a Russian human trafficking syndicate just for kicks.

He is also brilliant, shrewd, and devious. They say money makes the world go round. Well, Prince knows how to bring home the green. He has an ear for talent and knows how to stroke an ego. Head-Hunter Media is the most successful record production company in history. Whoever thought their predecessors would be replaced by a firm that didn't even exist just a few years before? Yes, the Illuminati is fortunate to have men like Elliot Prince. And Luckily there is more like him around.

William Davenport for instance. Wild Bill Davenport is president of Segrave-Hartman Pharmaceuticals. He was elected president by the company's board of directors even though he is a psychiatrist by trade. Davenport is the perfect example of someone being in the right place at the right time...

The folks who work on the company's research & development team had beaten the competition by being the first to develop a pill that would legitimately provide males with the ability to grow a larger penis. Having exclusive distribution rights to their new product for decades to come Segrave-Hartman needed to know the best way to market it. Fortunately for Bill Davenport that is precisely when he came on board.

Davenport was originally hired to provide company executives with insight into the male psyche, and he did a masterful job. Not only did the psychiatrist explain what drives male sexuality, he introduced the board to the idea of using subliminal messaging and thought control to affect their customers subconscious.

Using Davenport's (i.e.The Illuminati's) methods, Segrave-Hartman crammed their advertising campaign with subliminal messaging. Millisecond bursts of pseudo-sexual images appeared on viewers screens, far too quickly to be caught by the naked eye but not the human mind. Phallic symbolism, sadomasochism, pedophilia. It was all there, or was it?

Whether television viewers knew it or not Queen Ishtar herself visited their bedrooms for well over two years. She being the obvious choice considering what it was being advertised. After all Queen Ishtar is the Babylonian Goddess of Sexuality.

When Segrave-Hartman was named the single most successful pharmaceutical company in the world Bill Davenport got the credit. Whoever said Fortune 500 companies have got to be lead by gurus from the world of business and finance? Money is money. The greedy don't give a damn where it comes from.

The company owes their long term success to the United States Congress. It was thanks to recent changes made to federal patent laws that gave Segrave-Hartman exclusive rights to distribute their little green grow your penis pill. By law no other pharmaceutical company is allowed to distribute a similar product within the confines of the United States.

Of course it is really The Illuminati who should get all the credit. They are the ones who got Republican Congressmen Terrance Daily and John Galbraith to go against their friends and benefactors on the Religious Right and change their vote. It was sheer genius. Seven out of every ten American men over the age of twenty-one now has a Segrave-Hartman pill prescription, at twenty-five bucks a pop. Needless to say the pharmaceutical is pulling in some serious cash. The Illuminati takes a sizable cut off the top but nobody at Segrave-Hartman is complaining.

Not that The Illuminati hadn't pulled that same trick before. God knows they have. Over the years the Illuminati has used their persuasive powers time and time again to get desired legislation passed by the United States Congress. The organizations political action committee is headed up by a man named Tom Vanderson. Vanderson is a former republican senator from the Commonwealth of Massachusetts. He is currently the special envoy to the People's Republic of China. The man is one smooth politician, but he has the moral fortitude of a Heinrich Himmler. Tom Vanderson would launch a ballistic missile strike against a city full of innocent women and children without batting an eyelash if The Illuminati asked.

Tom's foray into politics started long ago. Back when he was a young buck he ran for Berkshire County Sheriff. His opponent had been some bible thumping goodie two shoes sheriff's lieutenant. Tom just couldn't imagine a wimpy Disciple of Christ in a job like that. Might as well open the jail house doors and step out of the way. Anyway, Vanderson, with the help of two sheriff deputy buddies, arranged a little sexual triad with the competition. The three of them convinced a heroin addict they'd busted to do what she does best. Prostitute herself for drug money. The dumb ass bible thumping sheriffs lieutenant couldn't resist.

Oh how the mighty do fall... Some people might suggest it has taken them two thousand years but they'd be wrong. Let me explain... Members of the Illuminati don't count time in years. Hell, they don't count time at all. To he who knows the truth there is no yesterday, today, or tomorrow. Time is but a concept. People are born, they hang around for a while, then they die... It's simply a matter of quantum physics.

Time is a paradox. An alternate reality. Our ancestors aren't people from the distant past. They are our brothers. Fellow dwellers in the continuum. All of that, *"God created the heavens and the earth"* crap is for the birds. It is what it is, plain and simple. You are either with them or you're against them...period.

Now take all of that with a grain of salt. Though time is a non issue The Illuminati does not intend to wait forever. It has taken centuries, that much is true...but things are coming along. There are people in place who will do what needs to be done when it needs to be done.

The Illuminati isn't naive. When the shit hits the fan they know full well there are those who won't walk the walk. But that doesn't matter. By then it will be too late. In the meantime they are all just waiting. They understand human beings are born into sin. The bible tells them so...

Since its early beginnings the Illuminati has elected one person to lead them. That person is known as The Pinnacle of the Draco. The Great Pindar. Today that person is a man named Stanton Price, Jr.

AN AMERICAN IDOL
The Illuminati Conspiracy

CHAPTER FIVE

Stanton Price, Jr. was in his fifties before he ever heard of the Illuminati. Even then it was strictly by chance. An officer of long standing with the Northern California Chapter of Freemasons, the wealthy mall developer was in New York City attending the Republican National Convention. He'd been selected as an elector for fellow freemason, California congressman Bill Barkel. Barkel was on the ticket after winning the California republican primary.

Stanton had made a substantial contribution to the congressman's election fund, which all but guaranteed him a spot as an elector. Three million dollars will buy you a ton of friends anywhere, but no more so then in the political arena.

Not that Stanton was all that interested in politics, other than how it affected his wallet. He didn't look at his contribution as a donation. To him it was an investment. An opportunity. A portal to power. Stanton Price, Jr. had always been a straight shooter. He saw the world in black and white, and he was prejudice as hell.

Not prejudice in the literal sense. Stanton's prejudice wasn't racially inspired. It was directed at those in society he viewed as weak. Limp wrist demagogues like that queer on CNN, or the billionaire tech freak hiding out in his mansion in the Redwood Forest. That bespectacled momma's boy was giving away all his money to feed the starving AIDS infected children of Africa no less. Better to let them all die of the disease, like their fourteen year old mothers.

But neither one of those men was considered worse than that latest equivocator of deceit, Pope Francis the talking mule. Stanton's hatred of the Holy Roman Catholic Church and its illustrious leader was firmly established long before he ever became a Freemason. As far as Stanton Price was concerned his holiness Pontifex Maximus was nothing more than a night-club bouncer in a white cassock. A lowlife Spic with a fancy title. Someday he hoped to show the 'Holy Seer' a side of himself few knew existed.

Stanton Price Jr, the King of California suburban strip malls, came from humble beginnings. His father was a Christian radio talk show host for WORD in Kansas City. The small 10,000 watt station had limited frequency. Listeners living within thirty miles of its tower could pick up a clear signal. For anyone beyond that distance it was hit or miss.

The Price family belonged to the Church of Christ. Stanton, Sr. was a self-professed hardline fundamentalist. He lorded over his home and all that dwelled within. That included his wife Elizabeth, two sons, Stanton, Jr. and Dwight, and a daughter, Rebecca Lynn.

Stanton Price, Sr. went by the call name Stanton the Elder. His twice daily radio program garnered accolades from the far right crowd in Kansas City. Back then there were quite a few of them in the area. Midwesterners tend to be on the conservative side anyway, so they were open to the ramblings of a hardline Holy-Joe preacher like Stanton the Elder.

You might be wondering what exactly it was that Stanton the Elder preached to his listeners over the radio twice a day, day in and day out, in Kansas City, Missouri. What limitations did he, by way of The Church of Christ, put on those who believed?

Well why don't we take a look and see.

* Consumption of alcohol is a sin
* Any kind of dancing is a sin
* A choir singing during a worship service is a sin
* Playing musical instruments during a worship service is a sin
* Clapping of hands during a worship service is a sin
* Using church funds to support an orphanage? You guessed it, sin

Stanton also told his listeners that gifts of the spirit have no place in the modern American church. He told them those who believe otherwise were being mislead, or worse, being dishonest.

Some of the radio preacher's rantings seemed downright silly. Like his insistence that all references to wine in the Bible are incorrect. Stanton the Elder insisted it was really grape juice they were all drinking. Of course he also insisted Jesus Christ was a white man with blondish brown hair. The truth is Jesus of Nazareth was a Palestinian Jew, with dark skin and dark black hair.

Some of Stanton's rantings weren't quite so silly. For instance he told listeners who may be suffering in abusive marriages that getting a divorce was not an option. God absolutely forbade divorce unless it was caused by the sexual sins of one's partner. He may as well have said one's wife because that's how it was received. Stanton

would then contradict himself by preaching that the only way for a previously divorced person to secure their place in heaven was if the spouse they sinned against would agree to remarry them. One can only imagine what it must have been like living in the Stanton Price home. I think I would prefer the Gulag, thank you very much!

If the old codger had been born a few years earlier he may have gotten away with it. Fortunately for the rest of us the 1970's happened. Elizabeth Stanton put up with her husband's domineering ways for twenty years before she finally couldn't take it anymore and left. When she did leave it was under the cover of darkness.

Elizabeth met someone. It happened several months before. The man's name was Peter Best. He was seven years younger than Elizabeth. A professor of American History at William Jewel University. The small liberal arts college was just down the road from the Price home.

Peter told Elizabeth he had no choice but to teach at William Jewel University. He was related to one of the school's founding fathers.

The Reverend Robert Salle James. Reverend James was his great grand uncle on his mother's side. Pete told her his great grand uncle also happened to be the father of outlaws Frank and Jesse James. Being an American history professor Pete was always surprising Elizabeth with unusual tidbits from our nation's history. Still this one was a bit much.

Stanton Price, Sr. had noticed a change in his wife's behavior the last few months of their marriage. It was incremental. At first she just didn't seem to jump as high when he said HOP. Then she began questioning his judgement, rather than accepting everything he said as gospel. Elizabeth Price was becoming the antithesis of God's interpretation of a wife. She was rebelling against her husband's God given authority, and it did not go unchallenged. The more Elizabeth rebelled the harsher her husband treated her.

Stanton blamed it on the times, and the inherent nature of women to sin. Eve's rebellion in the Garden of Eden wasn't by chance. It was a weakness formed in her very being. It was part of her DNA. The maternal mother of us all was at her very core, sinful.

The 1970's could be deemed the decade of feminine defiance. The Equal Rights Amendment was passed by the United States Senate. The Supreme Court ruled sex discrimination was a violation of a woman's civil rights. Roe v. Wade legalized a woman's right to have an abortion. The court later determined a woman didn't need her husband's consent to terminate a pregnancy. According to Stanton Price Jr. Satan had a stronghold over America. The entire country was heading to hell in a hand basket. One weaved by the feminine mystique.

Stanton's response to his wife's rebellion was clear and present. She was forbidden to watch any television. Forbidden to read magazine articles. His justification was simple. They were satanic. Neither was she allowed to speak at the dinner table, nor to her husband in front of their children. It was disrespectful. Elizabeth Price was a prisoner in her own home... But that didn't stop her.

Elizabeth happened to be walking in the park just down the street from her house when she first met Peter. The bushy haired professor was rolling around on the ground wrestling with a dog. It appeared to her the huge German Shepherd had attacked him. What really happened was Peter saw the woman coming and thought it would be funny if he feigned he was under attack. He later admitted it was a vain attempt to get her attention.

Elizabeth's uncharacteristic response could not have been planned. She actually bolted toward the aggressive animal and grabbed him by the collar. The two of them tumbled to the ground in a heap.

Pete found the woman who'd come to his rescue lying flat on her back with his fifty pound german shepherd laying across her chest. The panting dog looked up at him with playfulness in his eyes. The dog's glistening tongue hung from his mouth in anticipation of more rough play. When Pete called him off the dog barked, licked his chops, and leaped to his feet. Pete extended his hand to help his would be rescuer up and when she grabbed it a jolt of electricity shot through his fingertips.

Static electricity from rolling around on the ground? Perhaps... Pete apologized for his obviously immature behavior, adding he was glad she wasn't bitten. He would later confess it was he who had been bitten that day... By love!

Elizabeth could only laugh. Her involuntary reaction to seeing someone being attacked by a dog came as a complete surprise to her. The last thing she ever thought she'd do was tackle a fully grown German Shepherd. It was a good thing she wasn't bitten!

They walked together as Pete's dog ran ahead. He told Elizabeth he was a professor at the college, and that he was divorced. He admitted he had seen her coming and thought it might be fun to watch her reaction. It never occurred to him she'd join the fray. As they reached the entrance to the park Pete asked if he could see her again. Elizabeth immediately closed her fist to conceal her wedding ring, then answered yes.

At first it was all rather innocent. Pete and his dog would meet Elizabeth in the park and they would walk together. Patton, Peter's dog, and Elizabeth became good friends. Pete knew if his dog liked this lady she must be okay. On their third visit he and Elizabeth held hands, on the fourth they kissed. On the fifth, she was his.

This went on for several months. Elizabeth would sneak out in the middle of the day, knowing her husband was occupied with his work. It was easy to keep tabs on him. Stanton the Elder's show was broadcast live from the WORD Radio studios.

When the time came to finally leave her husband Elizabeth knew she was doing the right thing. The marriage was over. When a woman cringes at the touch of her husband it's a telltale sign. Still she was frightened. Stanton Price was a deceptively strong man, and had a low tolerance for disloyalty. The woman didn't know how he would react, but she knew what he was capable of.

Peter wanted to confront the issue head on like mature adults. He felt the three of them could talk it out. After all what man would want a wife who didn't want him? He had let his go, why not Stanton?

Elizabeth knew better. If she'd learned anything in twenty years it was that you don't reason with Stanton the Elder. Stanton did not negotiate. He did not dicker. It was God's way or the highway.

Stanton, Jr. was fifteen when his mother left. His sister was fourteen, and his brother, twelve. Stanton hated his mother for leaving. He blamed her for destroying their family. What kind of woman walks out on a devoted, God fearing man like his father? What mother would leave her children to be with a pot smoking hippie? Especially one so much younger than her. How could she do this to him? To them?

It is true the family, at least individually, was destroyed. Elizabeth couldn't have known her husband would spend the rest of his life a cold, misery ridden recluse. A man who would come to be despised by people. People he took advantage of and left without hope. A man who would refuse to offer anyone a condolence or good will. Stanton the Elder would die twelve years after his wife left. His funeral was attended by just three people. His former employer at WORD radio. His old minister at the Church of Christ, who himself would pass away two weeks later, and his eldest son and namesake.

Rebecca Price, Stanton the Elder's fourteen year old daughter, ran away from home six months after her mom did. Elizabeth Stanton fully understood why. She only wished Rebecca had come to her. She and Pete had discussed making their home available to her children if they ever wanted to come. They agreed not to push it on them but the option was there if they ever wanted to come. Many years later she learned Rebecca had gone to California in search of truth.

Upon arriving in California Rebecca had tried to find work, but with little luck. The teenage runaway stayed at a youth hostel in Fresno where she met friends. Friends who got her involved in drugs. After acquiring an impossible to satisfy taste for heroin Rebecca took to selling herself on the street to feed her habit. The next couple years took their toll. At the age of seventeen Rebecca ended up in a court ordered rehab program. That's where she met the man she'd spend the rest of her life with.

Charles Cook was himself a recovering heroin addict. After accepting Christ as his personal savior he started volunteering at the Stockton Center for Personal Growth every other weekend. Ten years older than Rebecca, Charles seemed wise and stable. Something she missed and yearned for. She made the first move.

As it turned out Charles Cook was neither wise nor stable. A master of deception, Cook was in truth less stable than Rebecca was. After succumbing to the teenage heroin addict's advances Charles led Rebecca down a twenty year path of self discovery that would eventually claim both their lives.

They bounced from Pentecostal church to Pentecostal church. From belief to belief. Before finding Christ Charles had tried Buddhism. Before that, Shinto. After being asked to leave one church by a pastor who caught him in a compromising position with his wife, Charles became a holy roller. His stint with Jehovah's Witness lasted about a year, then it was off to yet another spiritual misadventure. He and Rebecca became disciples of Sun Myung Moon. They joined the Unification Church and were put to work as couriers for the Washington Times, a conservative newspaper started by the Moon God himself.

Other adventures followed. Charles and Rebecca even dabbled in the occult for a spell. Everything culminated in the early 1990's, when Charles and Rebecca moved to San Diego. That is where they met a new age philosopher named Marshall Applewhite.

Charles had taken a job with a Southern California newspaper publishing company that printed a popular alternative weekly called the 'Vigilant Thinker.' The rag, known in local circles as the VT, was available in bookstores and coffee houses throughout the San Diego area. One day the newspaper ran a story about new age philosophy, and they interviewed Marshall Applewhite.

Applewhite had appeared on numerous local television talk shows and was well known throughout Southern California. He was a purveyor of the historical astronaut argument. Applewhite believed earth was visited by extraterrestrials millions of years ago. These alien beings supposedly planted the seeds of modern humanity. The Vigilant Thinker newspaper ran a series of articles about Applewhite and his group, Heaven's Gate.

Eventually, one might even say predictably, Charles and Rebecca joined Heaven's Gate. On March 20th, 1997 they both appeared alongside Marshall Applewhite as he videotaped an announcement for later broadcast. Heaven's Gate was going to conduct a mass suicide, asserting the earth was about to be wiped clean by its alien propagators.

Suicide was the only way Applewhite and his group could evacuate the earth. He claimed he and his followers were going to meet up with the alien mother-craft, which would transport their souls, and I quote, "To a level of existence above human." You can't make this stuff up folks. I'm just telling you the way it was.

A week later Charles and Rebecca were dead. Their rotting decomposed corpses were discovered in an upstairs bedroom in a suburban mansion in Rancho Sante Fe along with thirty-seven other fellow cultists. The medical examiner determined the cause of death to be asphyxiation. Each one of them had swallowed a phenobarbital laced pineapple juice cocktail and placed a plastic bag over their heads.

Truth? At the tender age of fourteen Rebecca Price had run away from home in search of truth. Elizabeth had been the recipient of a letter from her missing daughter twenty years earlier. It arrived three days after she originally disappeared. In that letter Rebecca offered 'A search for truth' as her reason for leaving. When word of the mass suicide conducted by the misguided members of Heaven's Gate was reported on national television Elizabeth pulled her daughter's letter out and reread it. Rebecca had written to her mother all those years ago hoping her words would ease her mother's pain. Hoping to some way dissipate her mother's anxiety and free her from worry. The letter read as follows:

"Dear Momma, I am writing this letter because I don't want you to worry about me. I'm a big girl now. A woman, really. I understand you did what you had to do, and so did I. Living with daddy has become unbearable. I think he blames me for what happened. He forbids me to watch television or talk on the phone. I'm not even allowed go outside, except to school."

"He's real mean to Dwight too. I worry about him. Daddy got mad at Dwight the other day and dragged him downstairs. He tied his wrists to the metal pole in the basement. The one you said supports the weight of the house. Daddy left him there all day long. The only thing Dwight did was take too long in the bathroom. Stanton says it was because dad caught him masturbating... He's such a liar!"

"Momma, I'm sorry I didn't say goodbye. Please forgive me. I wish you and that man you are with all the happiness. You deserve some

*before you die. As for me, I'm going in search of truth.
Your loving daughter, Becky."*

Elizabeth openly weeped as she read it. Tears of suffering for one's own mistakes. Guilt follows you to the grave, especially when it's rooted in blood. Had she been given another chance to do things differently, would she have? Perhaps. That's the thing about life. You only get one go round.

Elizabeth's youngest child didn't fare much better than his sister. She knew in her heart she shouldn't have left him. Dwight never could do anything right in his father's eyes. Stanton, Sr. never laid a finger on his oldest son, or his daughter for that matter, but Dwight...that was a different story. Spare the rod and spoil the child. When it came to Dwight that was Stanton the Elder's motto.

When Rebecca ran away from home she took a part of Dwight with her. After his mother ran off the boy's big sister was his rock. He went to her for everything. Advice, help with his homework, a hug. Dwight was truly lost without her. He hung on for a while. Though his mental condition was precarious Dwight was able to cope. He went through his daily rituals without to much trouble, but inside he was a ticking time bomb waiting to explode.

His father took no mercy. Stanton knew his son was suffering. He hated him for his weakness. "Be a man for Christ sake," he would say. "Stop whimpering like a little baby…and leave your willy alone... You'll go blind... I'm warning you!" Then there was the forever ongoing reminder. "Why can't you be like your brother?"

What was he to do? Dwight could only think of one plausible answer. He'd crawl up inside himself and hide. He'd pull the old duck and run. He'd live his life in the shadows. You can't hurt what you can't see, right? But it didn't work. His teachers rode his back for not participating in class. Other kids avoided him because he was "weird." His brother pretended he didn't even exist. Bullies at school saw it as an opportunity. Nobody cared about this dope. Let's use him as a whipping post. Dwight was crucified, sans the cross.

During his sophomore year in high school something changed. Oh, but it had been building. After all one can only take so much. How many times can the rotten little prick who sits behind you in class whack you over the head with his notebook when the teacher isn't looking? How often can bullies force you to cough up your lunch money to avoid having the shit kicked out of you after school? How many girls can point and laugh when they see you walking towards them? Dwight had seen 'Carrie.' Stephen King had all the answers in that movie. If only he had that power. If only...

Dwight couldn't telekinetically start a fire and burn his high school down with all the other kids inside. He couldn't flip his teacher's car over and make it explode or cause his house to come crashing down on top of his father while the old bastard slept in his bed. He couldn't nail his mother to a cross...

He could however scare the shit out of the lot of them. Dwight rummaged through his father's closet until he found the Winchester Springfield he knew was hidden there. The old 30 aught 6 would do his speaking for him. They'd listen then. They fucking well better...

Fortunately...unfortunately...he was denied. The police officer who shot Dwight told reporters he personally knew the youngster. He and his wife went to the same church as the boy's parents. He said he understood the Price's had recently split up. "I gave the kid an opportunity to drop his weapon," the officer explained. "I promised we'd get him some help. When the youngster turned his rifle on me I saw the look in his eyes. I said me a little prayer, then fired."

Besides Dwight, two other kids died in the rampage. Another two were wounded while running for help. Dwight didn't know any of his victims. They were just kids that went to his school. Kids that happened to be in the wrong place at the wrong time. They had no way of knowing Dwight was carrying around all that anger. That kind of anger has no reason. It doesn't use logic, or common sense. It just acts on impulse. The cop who shot Dwight would have been added to the list of dead if he hadn't stopped him.

Stanton, Sr. tried to act as though his son's atrocity was a result of the sins committed by his unfaithful wife. He wrapped himself in the condolences of his church family, many of whom were more than willing to blame the entire tragedy on her too. The following Sunday his pastor preached on the long lasting effects of sexual sin in America, quoting scripture after scripture as a point of reference. He didn't bother quoting any of the scriptures dealing with being a loving husband and father though.

After her daughter ran away and her son was killed Elizabeth knew she couldn't stay in Kansas City any longer. Losing one child was heartbreaking. Losing two was worse than death. Pete took a leave of absence from William Jewel College and he and Elizabeth went on sabbatical. Pete had a sister who taught english at a university in Costa Rica. They decided to go there.

Stanton, Jr. became the apple of his father's eye. Not that he hadn't been anyway, but considering his other two children had disappointed him so it was comforting to know at least his namesake had a good head on his shoulders. He made sure the boy stayed on the straight and narrow, encouraging him to focus on his studies and make something of himself. Even though his income dropped after the shooting, as a result of a drop in his radio audience market share, Stanton made sure his surviving son wanted for nothing.

Stanton, Jr never had to work after school like many of his friends. He didn't have to save for a car or worry about buying new clothes. He didn't have to earn money so he could ask a girl out on a date. Stanton, Jr. never saw the working side of a Burger King counter. His dad paid for everything. All he had to do was excel at school and not embarrass him.

Dad would be proud of him now. After graduating with honors from Pepperdine University Stanton Price Jr. decided to remain on the West Coast. He took a job as a new construction marketing strategist with the Southern California Building Association. The position put him in direct contact with some of the industries leading contractors, suppliers, and investment bankers. Stanton held seminars, arranged trade shows, and made acquaintances.

Like his father, Stanton never was one to make friends. They were acquaintances. People you might share something in common with but know they will eventually let you down. Stanton learned to use people to his advantage. Milk the cow until the bucket is full then move to the next cow. That's the way Stanton's father used to put it.

Stanton did have one acquaintance he maintained a relationship with. A guy he met in college named Michael Charm. Michael came from a similar background as Stanton. He was also a child from a broken home, and his father was a devout Christian fundamentalist too. Stanton remembers the day Michael Charm exercised his free will and pried himself free from his father's firm grip. It was an eye opening event.

The two definitely took different paths. Michael Charm became a dedicated agnostic. He was a year ahead of Stanton at Pepperdine, but in the same field of study. They met while rehearsing for a video presentation each had to give as part of the course curriculum. Both young men saw themselves as successful marketeers, and both possessed an inner drive to succeed.

It was Michael Charm who introduced Stanton to the inconceivable idea that God might not exist. Up to then Stanton was pretty damn sure of his religious beliefs. After all they'd been drilled into his head since birth.

"Our God is a loving God, but he is fiercely jealous in his demand for loyalty," Stanton's father taught him. "The Lord Jehovah breathes an all consuming fire, and his vengeance is eternal...Those who arouse God's anger will suffer the consequences."

Stanton, Sr used quotes like those time and again to instill fear in his children. He even suggested Stanton would pay for the adulterous behavior of his mother. "The sins of the parents will be visited upon the children, even unto the fourth generation."

Stanton didn't leave the church then, but would several years later after marrying a divorcee. Shelly Donatelli was a very good looking twenty-eight year old Italian lady Stanton met at a conference he attended up in Lake Tahoe. She'd been divorced for five years, and had no children. Being catholic Shelly knew she'd be required to have her first marriage declared invalid by the church before being allowed to remarry. That wasn't a problem, or it shouldn't have been.

The problem only arose when Stanton discovered having Shelly's marriage annulled by a priest would cost her five-hundred dollars. Some bullshit called a decree of invalidity. Without it she could still attend mass, but she wouldn't be allowed to take the blessed sacraments or partake in holy communion.

It wasn't about the money. Shelly had a good job. She was an assistant producer on a reality television show currently in its fifth year on the air. Stanton himself was pulling down two hundred grand a year as a marketing strategist. No, it wasn't money. It was the principal of the thing. Shelly had been divorced for five years. Now the Catholic Church wanted her to buy her freedom? Fuck that.

Stanton wanted his future wife to convert to the Protestant religion anyway. Yes members of the Church of Christ were expected to tithe, but they weren't forced to buy their salvation. Only when Stanton mentioned the issue to his father did he realize his bride to be wouldn't be welcome in his church either.

It wasn't because Shelly was Catholic. The Church of Christ would gladly steal a soul away from a religious institution they considered a cult. The teachings of the Catholic Church were an abomination unto the Lord as far as they were concerned. No it was because she was divorced. Even worse she had initiated the divorce. Nowhere in

Shelly's divorce decree had her husband been cited for committing any unacceptable offenses. He'd simply agreed to part ways. After a year of legal separation their divorce was granted.

That, according to Stanton Price, Sr...would bar her from joining the Church of Christ. The only way she could become a member would be to remarry her previous husband. The idea being they were still husband and wife in the eyes of God. It didn't matter what the Superior Court of California decreed.

That was that. Stanton was out. He wasn't welcome by the Vatican, and his bride wasn't welcome in the Church of Christ. Damn them all. Stanton called his friend Michael Charm and told him what he was doing. Two months later he and Shelly were card carrying members of Skeptics United. Michael Charm's fifty-thousand member non-profit consortium for the advancement of scientific methodology and critical thinking.

The consortium included nationally recognized leaders from the fields of science and technology, journalism, finance, and higher education. The membership included government policy makers, bankers, insurance executives, and business owners. The music and film industry was well represented too, as was politics. Skeptics United was a bubbling cauldron of well heeled intellectuals who saw themselves as the answer to the world's problems.

Stanton eventually became Presidium of the California chapter.
Nearly twelve years passed before he began to question what it was he actually believed in. Skeptics United was founded on the principal that man is the answer to his own impermanence. Humanity will survive until it chooses not to. The end will come not as a fulfilled prophesy or because some invisible God somewhere chose to unleash his wrath upon the earth. It will come because of mankind's failure to endure. To be an honest to goodness skeptic is to not believe in the supernatural, or in the existence of something bigger than one's self. After twelve years Stanton began to question those beliefs.

Most everyone change their views on life as they age. Democrats become Republicans. Left wingers come closer to the center of the political pie. Nonbelievers start to question their own mortality. They start to wonder if perhaps there is a God after all. Stanton Price, Jr. was certain the future was already predetermined, he just didn't know who or what controlled it. In his quest for answers he discovered Freemasonry.

Stanton found his true calling there. Successful businessmen were seen as natural leaders in the Freemasons. In just his seventh year Stanton Jr. rose to the twenty-fifth level of Freemasonry and became a Chevalier of the Brazen Serpent.

AN AMERICAN IDOL
The Illuminati Conspiracy

CHAPTER SIX

When Will Durance left the medical examiner's office he drove straight to the police station. He was hoping someone might have filed a missing persons report or a witness to the suicide had come forward, but no one had. Being Christmas things were relatively quiet. The detective went down to the break room and dropped a couple quarters in the coffee machine, all the while wishing the donut shop he normally visited every morning had been open. Like pretty much everything else Donut World was closed for the Christmas holiday.

There was a flat screen TV mounted on the wall in the break room. It normally ran twenty-four seven but with a skeleton crew working the holiday the television was off. Will was about to turn it back on when his cell phone rang. It was Dr. Rupert. The medical examiner had done some more tests. When he ran his analysis through the computer database he got a positive ID on the suicide victim. Rupert told Spider he was not going to believe what he was about to hear.

The dead bloated body the Daytona Beach Police Department had hauled back onto the pier earlier that morning was an extremely famous rock musician. None other than multi-platinum recording artist and recent American Idol winner Jeremy London. Spider was flabbergasted. He asked the medical examiner if anyone else knew about his findings. Rupert answered, "Negative... Nobody." Will suggested he keep it under wraps, at least for a little while. The police chief would need to be notified, as would Dr. Rupert's boss. Will was quite certain his chief would want to make a public announcement. He stood there contemplating his next move. Being a young homicide detective in Daytona was not easy. Not by a long shot.

Chief Sparks was not happy when he found out Will was calling him at home on Christmas morning. Will apologized profusely, explaining he would not have interrupted him if it wasn't completely necessary. When Sparks heard why his detective called him he changed his tune. Fuck the Christmas presents. His kids would have to wait a little longer. This was big... National Headlines Big!

Will knew Jeremy London was a local boy. His story had been featured in the News-Journal a couple years back when the young singer reached the American Idol television show's Live sessions.

The New Smyrna Beach native had made quite a splash on the talent show. The local newspaper article mentioned Jeremy London grew up in New Smyrna Beach and had worked for Hell On Wheels Motorcycle Parts up in Flagler County. The article went on to say London had transferred to the facility in Cedar Rapids, Iowa when the parts distributor cut its local staff last year.

Spider Will owned two Jeremy London albums himself. The singer's latest CD, Celluloid, had recently been nominated for a Grammy Award.

A quick check told the detective Jeremy London still had family in the area. His parents lived in New Smyrna Beach, out by the recently opened Walmart on State Route 44. He also learned why the singer was in Florida. Jeremy had a television special scheduled for that night. The concert was coming from Main Street USA in Disney World on Christmas night. It was supposed to be broadcast live on pay per view. That fact made Will's job inherently harder. Bad enough he had to make a public announcement. With Disney in the picture and a Christmas night audience with no one to entertain them things would be crazy. People would come to Daytona just to visit the site of their idol's tragic death.

Will had read about people who still visit Jim Morrison's burial site in Paris. People who flock to Jimi Hendrix burial site outside Seattle to pay their respects. Both sites pale when compared to Strawberry Fields in New York City's Central Park or Elvis Presley's Graceland. Spider had no doubt the Daytona Beach Pier would be selling tickets. He asked to have someone from the department's victim advocate office accompany him to the London home. When he went to share the news of Jeremy's death with the singer's parents he wanted somebody there who was trained to deal with that kind of situation. Spider knew people are often shocked when they heat the have lost a loved one. When it's a child it is even worse.

In this case the news would be doubly tragic. For one thing the death was a suicide. Furthermore news of his demise would be gossip fodder for every single newspaper reporter and television newscaster in the country. Once the news came out the London family's New Smyrna Beach home would be besieged by paparazzi.

Will got lucky. Carmella Henson was the advocate on call that day. Carmella was the most experienced advocate the department had. The divorced former policewoman had seen it all over the years. Will had worked with her eight months before on a murder investigation. Carmella had concentrated on helping the perpetrators family while Spider scurried through their home looking for evidence.

Though the killer had been murdering women in and around the Daytona Beach area for fifteen years the guy had a clean record. He'd never even been issued a traffic citation. By all accounts the man was an upstanding husband and father. He even supported his elderly mother, who lived in an apartment her son had built on the back of his home five years before.

The murderer was always building something in his backyard. First a shed then a small greenhouse for his wife. He even installed a wine cellar along the side yard. At least that's what he told his Mrs. When she informed her husband she'd called a plumber because water wouldn't drain from the bathtub and a nasty smell was coming from the wine cellar the woman found out what he was really up too.

The man happened to be on a week long fishing expedition with some of his buddies when his wife called him. They were making their way down the St Johns River from Sanford to near Titusville. Along the way he and his pals would fish the river's back channels and sloughs for crappies and shad. When they hit deeper water they'd switch out their bait and fish for large mouths bass. The fish would be spawning for another month or two.

When he found out his wife had called in a plumber he went nuts. The woman was used to her husband's temper tantrums but this one was unlike any she'd been forced to bear before. Like most couples they'd had arguments, but nothing like this. The man called his wife every filthy name in the book. He insisted she call the plumber and cancel the appointment right then and there. He'd take care of the problem when he got home.

She was specifically told not to let anyone go near his wine cellar. When his wife asked him why the man blew a gasket. He threatened to beat her to death if she let anyone near that cellar.

That was enough to churn the butter. Don't ever tell a woman she can't do something. Not unless you want her to do it. When the guy threatened his wife with bodily harm if she went near his wine cellar he dug his own grave. The first thing she did after hanging up the phone was go searching for the key.

She found it hidden in her husband's sock drawer. The key was stuffed under a thick pile of porno magazines she didn't know he stashed there. With key in hand she made her way to the side of the house and unlocked the semi-submerged cellar door.

The smell coming from her backed up bath tub was mild compared to the stench she inhaled when she opened that door. First thing the woman saw was two decomposing corpses. They were hanging from meat hooks impaled high on the cement block wall. Both bodies were dressed in cheap, partially torn lingerie. A sticky pile of goo littered the dirt floor below them. When something slithered through it the woman quickly slammed the door shut and ran back inside the house.

The entire event came to light because of that one conversation the woman had with her husband. He actually showed up a few hours later to find homicide detectives tearing up his backyard. Carmella was inside comforting his wife, his mother, and his two children.

The guy walked in the house acting dumb as a rock. Carmella later suggested he wasn't acting. He feigned complete surprise, claiming he had no idea how two dead bodies ended up in his wine cellar. Needing to provide a distraction for the kids Carmella put a Disney video in the family's DVD player. The youngsters watched 'Pirates of the Caribbean' while the three women sat at the kitchen table drinking coffee and crying together.

Amazingly three additional bodies were dug up that night. Another was discovered buried behind the auto body shop the guy worked at over in Holly Hill. Personal items belonging to each of the woman were found inside the home. Jewelry that the killer had given to his wife as gifts, as well as several of the victims driver's licenses. Even some of the panties in the wife's lingerie drawer actually belonged to the murdered women.

Carmella handled the entire affair with professional compassion. She even added the killer's children to the police department's 'Helping Hands' Christmas program. Will was certain she'd be a great comfort to Jeremy London's family too. They were sure to be devastated by the horrific news. He drove.

June London was in the kitchen putting icing on a fresh batch of Christmas cookies when the front doorbell rang. Her husband was knocking a golf ball around the living room. He'd bought himself a new putter for Christmas. After taking a final shot he leaned the club against the wall and went to answer the door. June could hear him mumbling that it was too early for the neighbors they'd invited over for dinner to arrive.

The London's didn't have many close friends. Ever since their son hit the big time people acted differently towards them. Jeremy was world famous, and wealthy beyond words. They weren't. The fact he paid off their mortgage was not indicative of the family's true dynamics. If anything they were dysfunctional. A paid off mortgage didn't alter that fact.

June and Larry London barely spoke to each another. They didn't argue or bicker. They just didn't fit. That was obvious the moment Mr. London answered the door. *"Can I help you,"* the burly man cooly asked the detective? *"We're expecting guests. What is it?"*

Will flashed his badge and identified himself as a police detective, then asked if he could come in. Once inside Spider told Mr. London he needed to speak to him and his wife together. Before Larry could summon June to the living room she walked out of the kitchen carrying a platter of warm cookies. She took one look at Will's badge and dropped the holiday inspired cookie tray on the tile floor. It was as if she'd read Will's mind. *"It's my Jeremy... What's happened to my son?"*

Carmella rushed to the distraught woman's side. Taking June's hand she led her to the sofa. Larry London just stood there staring at Will, as if waiting for him to deny his wife's assumption. He didn't.

"Mr. and Mrs. London... I am regrettably here to inform you of your son's... I mean to say, he's been... Look I'm very sorry... Jeremy is dead. Your son's body was found early this morning. It appears he may have taken his own life."

Larry London didn't move a muscle. He didn't even flinch. June was stunned silent for a moment too. Then the traumatized woman let out a horrific scream. Carmella squeezed the grieving mother's hand and whispered something in her ear. Whatever it was the victim advocate said to her appeared to settle the woman down long enough Will could continue with his official duties.

"We were able to identify your son through his fingerprints," he informed them. "You should know the medical examiner has ruled out foul play. Your son apparently hung himself. His body was discovered by a citizen who was fishing down by the Daytona Beach Pier early this morning."

Mr. London walked over to where his wife had dropped the cookie platter and started picking up the ones that weren't broken. After gathering them up he carried the platter into the kitchen then just seemed to disappear.

June London thanked Carmella for being compassionate, mistakenly referring to her as 'Detective.' Carmella corrected her, explaining what it was she does. *"I am just a victim advocate, Mrs. London. If you need help notifying family members, or making funeral arrangements. Whatever it is you need we want to help. You are not alone, June... Okay?"*

She pulled a business card from her shirt pocket and placed it on the sofa table. *"Anything you need, just call. We have a list of very compassionate grief counselors. We can assist you with funeral arrangements. We can help you try and dig through the volumes of paperwork you are sure to be inundated with. I'm sure your son has personal items you'll want to claim. We can help with that too."*

Carmella stood and walked over to rejoin her colleague. She nodded to him, indicating they should probably leave. Will put up a finger, then turned to face the grieving mother and said, *"Ma'am, Your son was a gifted musician. I have several of his CD's myself. I'm sure the world will miss him. I should warn you though, when word of Jeremy's death gets out your home is going to be besieged by the press. Unless you are emotionally ready to deal with paparazzi poking microphones in your face and following you everywhere you might want to consider making alternate arrangements. Just some friendly advice."*

Then the detective turned around and headed for the door. When he reached it he turned back around again and said, *"Please give my deepest sympathies to your husband, Mrs. London. I'm sure this has come as quite a shock to you both."*

June London followed her visitors out. Spider was about to get into his squad car when the grieving woman grabbed his arm and calmly but resolutely announced, *"My son did not kill himself, Detective. Jeremy was murdered... He was happy...and very rich. My son did not commit suicide...That fucking demon murdered him!"*

AN AMERICAN IDOL
The Illuminati Conspiracy

CHAPTER SEVEN

Will dropped Carmella off at the station but didn't go inside himself. It was almost two o'clock in the afternoon. All he wanted to do was go home so he could crawl in bed and bury his head under the covers. The detective closed his eyes and leaned back against his car's headrest. If it hadn't been for the sound of someone blaring their horn Spider might have fallen asleep right there in the police department parking lot. The short blast startled him a little. When he sat up to see who was beeping at him he saw it was Carmella. She motioned for the young detective to roll his window down. *"You look like you could use a stiff drink, Detective,"* she hollered. *"Why don't you follow me... I make a great dirty martini."*

Will was more than a little surprised. He never expected Carmella Henson would invite him over for a drink. The senior victim advocate was at least fifteen years his senior. Don't get me wrong. Carmella is a good looking woman, but fifteen years is fifteen years. That put her in her sophomore year of college when Will was just entering kindergarten. It did cross his mind the woman's invitation might be completely innocent.

"Ummm... Okay," he responded. Carmella lived ten minutes from the station. Will followed her home, albeit somewhat hesitantly. Before he got out of his car the detective reminded himself to be on his best behavior. If he was misreading this entire scenario he didn't want to come off looking like some horny wolf hoping to take advantage of a lonely divorcee. On the other hand he was a horny wolf...

The detective offered to hold Carmella's purse as she fumbled to unlock the front door. Once inside she reclaimed her purse and placed it under the dining room table. Then she turned to Will and told him to make himself comfortable while she freshened up.

While waiting for his hostess/coworker to return Will admired the small, five foot tall artificial Christmas tree Carmella had on display in the corner of her living room. It was tastefully decorated with unique one of a kind ornaments and just the right amount of tinsel. He hadn't bothered with a tree this year. Seeing Carmella's left him wishing he had. He noticed there were two freshly unwrapped gift boxes at the base of the tree. Oh but to have a detective's intuition for the tiniest of details.

Spider turned his attention to the gorgeous paintings displayed on Carmella's living room walls. He'd always been something of an art history buff. Especially when it came to the postimpressionist era. Spider could tell the victim advocate had an artist's eye. Hanging above her gas fireplace was an amazingly accurate print of Georges Lemmen's, *'The Beach at Heist.'* Will was familiar with the artist's work. He'd seen the original of this one prominently displayed in the Musee d'Orsay in Paris.

There was a contemporary white leather sofa opposite the fireplace. Just above it hung the George Seurat work, *'Le Chahute.'* The piece was one of Seurat's last paintings. The French artist completed the burlesque themed masterpiece a year before his death in 1891.

Diametrically opposite this work was the controversial *'Fate of the Animals,'* by German artist Franz Marc. The colorful replica hung on the wall in Carmella's dining room. The painting is said to portray the tension of impending cataclysm in Germany at the time the artist painted it. The original is on permanent display at the Kuntz-Musee in Basel, Switzerland. Franz Marc enlisted in the German army at the outbreak of World War I. He was killed by exploding shrapnel during the Battle of Verdun.

Spider was completely absorbed in the painting when Carmella entered the room. She was wearing a shimmering neon black shift dress and tall sparkly sandals. When Will turned to acknowledge her presence he noticed she had taken her hair down. He'd only seen Carmella with her hair pinned back. The effect was quite intoxicating.

"So, how about that Martini, Detective," his accommodating hostess asked, *"or would you prefer a cold beer?"*

Though Spider truthfully did prefer cold beer over a martini he knew Carmella would be disappointed if he said so. *"I'll stick with the Martini, thank you,"* he answered.

A look of satisfaction slowly appeared on Carmella's face. It was like the misty fog you see on a car's windshield when you first start the engine on a cool morning. To her way of thinking making the perfect martini was a learned skill. *"Martini it is then,"* she responded. *"Shall I make it dirty?"*

Will assumed the one time police officer turned victim advocate was toying with him now. He sensed it. *"I like it a little dirty,"* he answered. *"In fact he dirtier the better, Ma'am..."*

Carmella suggested her guest take a seat on the sofa. She lit the gas fireplace and put on some soft jazz before disappearing into the kitchen. Will noticed a gossip magazine lying on a side table and grabbed it. After flipping through the pages for awhile he put it down and closed his eyes. The man was exhausted.

When he finally came to hours later the entire house was dark but for the Christmas tree. At first discombobulated Will soon remembered where he was, though the circumstances were a bit sluggish. He recalled sitting down on Carmella's white leather sofa while she went to fix them a drink. He remembered leaning back against the plush Italian leather and closing his eyes. Spider hadn't meant to fall asleep, but he realized that is exactly what he did.

Will had refused to allow himself to imagine spending the night with Carmella, though secretly he had hoped he might. This wasn't quite

how he envisioned it happening though. He could hear his hostess softly snoring in the bedroom. It was just down the hall. Carmella was breathing heavily in her sleep. Spider likened it to the purring of a kitten. He wondered if she was dreaming. He knew he had.

In his dream Spider had fantasized Carmella was dragging her long red fingernails across his back as he prepared to penetrate her. Just as he was about to he was unceremoniously dragged back to reality by a long and exceedingly doleful *"MEEEOWWW."*

The mournful howl came from outside the house. Carmella's cat was in heat... The lustful paramour. At least that's what Will imagined. Two frosted martini glasses sat perched on the side table where the gossip magazine had been. One of the glasses was empty. The other half full. Spider stood up, stretched, then gulped down what remained of the half full glass. After a moment spent contemplating the situation the detective let himself out.

AN AMERICAN IDOL
The Illuminati Conspiracy

CHAPTER EIGHT

The following morning Spider happened to bump into Carmella Henson as she was stepping off the elevator. Their eyes met briefly before Will embarrassingly looked away. He wasn't sure why. He hadn't acted inappropriately the night before. He'd simply dozed off while waiting for his dirty martini. It had been a very long day. If anything negative came of it it was his manhood that got bruised. After all when opportunity knocks are men not supposed to run to answer the door. Not him. He'd run out it...

Then again the question remained had it in fact been an opportunity? Carmella Henson had simply invited a colleague over for a drink after they had spent a very stressful day together. A day performing a very burdensome duty. Under the circumstances a stiff alcoholic beverage was called for, was it not?

Spider almost said something to her as he stepped on the elevator but he remained silent. Just before the elevator doors closed he heard her ask, *"Did you get a good night's sleep, Detective?"*

Will felt himself blush a little as he held the elevator door ajar so it wouldn't close on him. Momentarily lost for words, the detective soon recovered. He stuck his head out into the hallway and said, *"Real sorry about that, Carm. Long day, you know. How about a rain check? My treat."*

"Okay, how about tonight then," she responded. *"Shall we plan on six o'clock. The Blue Grotto?"* She liked this kid. She hadn't invited him over to her house so she could seduce him. Not that she couldn't, but that hadn't been her intention at all. She just wanted to get to know him a little better, and fix him one of her special dirty martinis. It was Christmas Day and they were both alone. What could it hurt?

The long time victim advocate understood just how stressful police work could be, especially for detectives. At one time she'd been married to one. Back when she still wore the uniform. The marriage ended badly. Her ex had a compulsive personality and two vices he struggled to control. Women and gambling. Carmella could put up with the women. The gambling on the other hand had gotten really out of control. When they lost their house to pay off a gambling debt the marriage collapsed like a deck of poker cards.

She still had a soft spot for cops, and saw in Will Durance an honest and honorable, yet brutally lonely man. Carmella knew from past conversations that Spider had an appreciation for fine art. She'd been wanting to show him her collection. Truth is she was lonely too. Having a friendly conversation about the works of Seurat and Cezanne over a dirty martini would have been soothing to her soul.

One painting Spider didn't see that night was Carmella's canvas print of Toulouse-Lautrec's 'Femmes de Maison' (The Prostitute). She'd bought it at a museum in Dallas, Texas while visiting her brother. He was a criminal attorney in Dallas, and on the board of directors at the Museum of Art. Carmella was amazed to discover the city's art museum had a collection of postimpressionist paintings, which just happens to be her favorite genre. An authentic copy of Lautrec's masterpiece hangs on the wall over her bed just begging to be admired.

Asking the young detective over to her place for a drink after work had been a compulsive act. Had she actually had time to plan it she probably never would have asked. The last time she did anything like that she ended up married.

Suddenly someone downstairs buzzed for the elevator. Will had to make a decision. Let the elevator door close or jump off, so he jumped off. For a moment Will didn't move at all. He just stood there silently. Carmella thought he looked a lot like a window mannequin in a men's clothing store. Finally she asked him, *"Was that a yes then, Detective?"*

Once that was settled Will made haste for his office. When he got to his desk he found a manilla envelope from the medical examiner's office sitting there. Inside were a dozen or so 8X10 glossy photos of Jeremy London's bloated naked body taken at the scene. One of the photos was particularly repugnant. It showed the singer's contorted corpse splayed out on the old wooden pier with a tightly bound noose biting into his neck. On one side of his face an optic globe hung inches from its socket. The jelly filled organ held in place by a thick sinewy length of tendon. The eyeball appeared to be looking straight into the camera, and hence, directly at Will.

Spider put that photo aside and started fingering through the pile. The medical examiner had included a copy of his official report. Will saw the cause of death listed was as the doctor had stated during the examination. Suicide by hanging, in turn causing asphyxia and venous congestion. Jeremy London had basically suffocated himself to death.

Will's phone rang. it was his lieutenant. A brawl had broken out at a biker bar down on Ridgewood Avenue, and the owner happened to be the lieutenant's uncle. He wanted Spider down there ASAP. Three police units were already on the scene.

Even though Jeremy London's death was officially ruled a suicide Spider was still curious about the case. The fact he was a fan had peaked his interest, but that wasn't the only driving force. There was something about the young man's mother that caused him to question what happened. How adamant she was that her son's death was not self-inflicted.

Will was very well aware most people play the denial card when someone close to them commits suicide. Especially mothers. This felt different to him. Call it intuition, but Spider was convinced June London knew something. He stuffed the 8X10 glossies back in the manilla envelope and hustled out the door.

When Will arrived at the bar on Ridgewood Ave the owner was being tended to by an EMT. His injury was serious, but not life threatening. The perpetrator had sliced a deep gash into the right side of the man's face. That told Will the attacker was most likely left handed.

It would take dozens of stitches to close the wound. The EMT was urging the man to get into the ambulance so they could get him to an emergency room but the guy was reluctant to leave the scene. After some investigative work Will discovered why.

The proprietor lived in a ramshackle mobile home parked behind the main building. As Will approached the dilapidated trailer he noticed a strange smell coming from inside. The front door was closed, but it was not locked. Concerned someone inside could be in serious trouble Spider decided to follow his intuition rather than wait to get a search warrant. He approached with some trepidation. After banging loudly on the front door Will identified himself then burst in with his weapon drawn.

Spider found himself standing in a small grease covered kitchen. It appeared he was alone. He followed the pungent smell he originally noticed when outside to a room at the rear of the trailer. The door to the room was closed. Again the detective knocked loudly and identified himself. Then he turned the door handle.

What Will saw took him completely by surprise. Laying spread eagle across the kingsize bed was a ten foot long alligator, its underbelly sliced completely open. A large plastic bucket on the floor next to the bed was filled with the reptile's innards. A bloodied gut hook knife sat on top of the glistening pile. Will did a double take then took two steps back and quickly closed the door. *"What the fuck,"* he said aloud, shaking his head in disbelief. *"Just when you think you have seen it all."*

Spider would have walked away and let the blue boys deal with it but something else in the room had caught his eye. He'd seen a small safe sitting on the floor in the corner closet. Two foot tall by two foot wide. The safe was partially hidden by a dingy plaid drape that hung haphazardly from a thick curtain rod. He assumed that was what substituted for a closet door with these folks. The drape was too small for the opening, which is how Will noticed the safe in the first place. The detective took a deep gulp of pungent air then reentered the room.

The entire bedroom was heavily coated with the pungent salty smell. Will had only gotten a hint of it before. An alligator doesn't give off much of a smell when alive, but slice that smooth underbelly open and it's an entirely different matter. Will gagged but was able to catch himself before puking. He put the alligator carcass out of his mind and made a beeline for the corner closet.

Spider was surprised to find the small safe open. Inside he found a glass pickle jar stuffed with currency of different denominations. Lying next to the pickle jar was a handgun. Next to that a round plastic prescription pill bottle. The label indicated the bottle held a prescription for something called Ropinirole. After gathering up the items he'd been careful not to touch with his fingertips Will bolted out the door.

The detective had some pretty heavy experience dealing with illegal narcotics. He was certain the prescription bottle held what it said it held but just to be sure he cleared off some room on the cluttered kitchen table and poured the pills out. The tiny nuggets rolled around the tabletop in haphazard circles for what seemed like forever. Will likened them to a group of Shrine Circus clowns driving their tiny toy like scooters around in figure eight patterns at a Labor Day parade.

Using the tip of his pen to separate them Spider counted the pills. When he was finished he picked one of them up and slid it into a little plastic bag then dropped the bag in his jacket pocket. He'd ask the police lab to run an analysis.

Will used his pen to lift the snub nosed revolver up by the trigger. He knew the gun had recently been fired because he could smell the cordite. Spider pulled a larger baggie out of his other pocket and dropped the weapon into it. Then he sealed the bag. Yes, a good detective always comes prepared. Next came the pickle jar.

Will shook the contents of the pickle jar out onto the stained formica tabletop. A wad of cash spilled out. Spider counted over thirty-seven hundred dollars. Most of it in one hundred dollar notes.

On his way back to the bar Spider pulled out his cell phone and dialed Dr. Rupert. He wanted to ask the medical examiner if he knew what Ropinirole was used for. The neurologist told Will the drug was a dopamine agonist used to treat Parkinson's patients. He also told him the medication comes with a host of nasty side effects. Dizziness, drowsiness, and insomnia to name a few. He said it can't kill you, but some of the side effects can.

Dr. Rupert told Will at higher doses Ropinirole had also been known to cause or jumpstart certain types of psychiatric behavioral disorders in some people. Obsessive/compulsive disorders, unusual sexual disorders, even addiction to gambling. Courts had handed out significant monetary awards in cases won by clients whose attorneys proved their clients suffered undo injury.

The doctor tried to explain to Will how the drug works, and how it's possible the medication might cause someone to develop certain compulsions but he soon gave up. Suffice it to say there had been litigation on the matter.

In addition to the owner of the bar, two other people involved in the brawl were treated for injuries. One customer had his two front teeth knocked out while another suffered a broken nose. A third man, the one who supposedly started the brouhaha, was shot in the foot but he disappeared before the cops arrived. A leather loafer with a ragged bullet hole in it lay on the floor beneath the bar. Will Durance surmised it must belong to him.

Five hours after arriving on the scene the detective had a clear picture of the events leading up to the brawl. Besides the four injured parties, six other men were physically involved in the milieu. Another four were onlookers. Anyone comparing the testimony of those who were present would agree it was caused by a verbal disagreement between the bar's proprietor and the man who was shot in the foot.

As Will was able to surmise, the owner of the bar owed a South Florida loanshark a considerable amount of money. The loanshark had connections with a Russian gangster he knew. The Russian gangster in turn sent two of his gophers to collect what was owed. According to witnesses the guy who got shot was one of the gophers.

What happened was the guy started mouthing off to the owner of the bar, threatening him with bodily harm if he didn't pay up. Things got heated and fists started flying. A bunch of the bars regular customers came to the bar owner's aid, which didn't sit well with the other gopher, who up to that point had been a silent observer. This guy was clearly the muscle of the two. When he joined the fray the bar owner pulled out a snub nosed Smith and Wesson revolver he kept concealed under the bar and shot a round towards the ceiling.

The bar owner admitting firing the weapon, hoping to scare the two gophers off. Instead his Russian nemesis reached inside his jacket and pulled out a sheath knife, which he then used to carve a nasty gash into the side of the bar owner's face. Witnesses stated the proprietor then fired a second round in reaction to his being cut with the knife, but that he hadn't intentionally aimed the gun at anyone. That bullet that was fired ended up tearing through the second gopher's foot.

After the two Russian thugs took off the proprietor of the bar ran back to his trailer and hid his gun in a safe he kept in a back bedroom. Then he called his police lieutenant brother in law, Spider's commanding officer. That's when Will got the order to get down there.

The gun became police evidence. The thirty-seven hundred bucks Spider found rolled up in the pickle jar became police property. The Ropinirole prescription remained in the safe, which Spider left open a crack, just as he'd found it.

AN AMERICAN IDOL
The Illuminati Conspiracy

CHAPTER NINE

Stanton Price, Jr. worked hard to reach the upper echelon of the Freemasons. He spent over six months at the organizations National Lodge in Washington, DC where he served as the Supreme Grand Chevalier of the Brazen Serpent. Officially Stanton's duties were considered hospitable in nature. He was obliged to greet visiting dignitaries and provide them assistance in any way he could. His behavior had to reflect his position. Faithfulness and sense of duty were to be his mantra.

Freemasonry is in truth a fraternity within a fraternity. Neophytes and those considered undesirable for further advancement are simply not aware of the true calling of a Freemason. They mire in the lower levels of Masonic degree. Rarely do these men go beyond the third level. For them being a Freemason is an opportunity to enjoy social camaraderie. It is a public venue dedicated to education, moral ethics, and humanitarian concerns.

There is however a much higher calling. This 'invisible' inner brotherhood operates independent of its 'visible' counterpart. Everyone involved in Freemasonry is part of the outer 'visible' Order. Only those who rise through the hierarchy and dedicate themselves to the true doctrine of the elect are aware of the 'invisible' brotherhood.

To be accepted into this secret brotherhood is to discover truth. Once one has proven himself worthy he is allowed to learn about the mystery of mysteries. The ultimate answer to life's hidden secrets. The Arcanum Arcanorum, if you will.

Stanton Price, Jr. was already there. Some have to wait until they've gone through all thirty-two Masonic degrees before moving on to the Esoteric levels Stanton Price, Jr. has reached. He was approached by members of the 'Circle of Circles' on the day he was awarded his twenty-sixth degree with an invitation to join the Illuminati.

It is quite rare, but it has happened before. Some have been chosen prior to completing their ascension up the ladder. Level twenty-six had become a bifurcate for those deemed Illuminati material. Though the two organizations were inseparable the Illuminati was the stronger of the two. Not in number of members, or the ability to persuade through normal channels mind you. The Freemasons won that battle hands down. No, the Illuminati was the stronger of the two because of its commitment to finish what had been started at the beginning. The purpose of the inner brotherhood was too clear the path of any obstructions so the Illuminati could proceed.

The day Stanton Price Jr. became a member of the Illuminati he found himself in the presence of greatness. His wealth, however impressive, seemed paltry compared to the fortunes of some of his colleagues. He was now in the same league as the crown heads of nations. As important as any chairmen of a multinational corporation. Any renown figure from the world of high finance. The leader of one of the largest illegal drug cartels in the world roamed freely through the room, completely unfazed by the presence of the former Director of the U.S. Secret Service. Even Hans Sorbeut, the commissioner of the International Criminal Police Organization, was there.

The ICPO seemed rightly named. Under the leadership of Sorbeut the organization had put in place a foolproof method of trafficking human beings in and out of the nearly two hundred countries it represented. The ICPO's annual budget of eighty-million euros was easily dwarfed by the three hundred billion it helped take in. No one it appears was policing the International Criminal Police Organization. If anyone was, they'd surely failed.

Stanton's ascension through the hierarchy of the Illuminati was as rapid as his rise through the Freemasons had been. Once that level was attained there was no other degree to aspire to. That was all behind him now. The Illuminati was made up of a council of thirteen which oversees two sub-councils. At that level everyone is already on the same page anyway. Inflated egos and hurt feelings are nonexistent amongst the membership. This was the big leagues. You don't get called up unless you are ready. Stanton Price, Jr. was.

After completing a year dedicated to discovery and learning Stanton clearly understood the magnificence of the organization's mission. Mankind had been heading towards its ultimate fate for centuries. Some in the Illuminati had been bred and borne to assist the organization on its course. When the time came, and that time was near, all would be set right.

No more wars. No more sickness. Hunger would be a thing of the past, as would poverty. No one left on the face of the earth would want for anything. No one would be on the face of the earth who didn't belong there.

Political affiliations, national pride, man-made boundaries meant to divide and separate, none of that would exist. Crime wouldn't exist. There'd be no need. Neither would money, at least in its present form. Religion would be exposed for what it really is. A man-made device concocted to frighten people into servitude. The Roman Catholic Church and its minions would be summarily booted out. It would be the final crucifixion of Christ!

The world would be united as it was meant to be. One world. One government. One people. All would bow to the truth. All would learn and except how it is they came to be. The world would take its rightful place and the power of the universe would reclaim his rightful place. And he would rule for eternity.

The lies and deceit of the ages would be exposed. With the light turned on the world will be illuminated to the truth. The time is coming, but there is work to do. The huddled masses remain lost. Most have no business being here. Earth wasn't meant to support eight billion people. It can't. We were given the technology to self correct that problem, but no one has had the guts to implement it... Until now!

AN AMERICAN IDOL
The Illuminati Conspiracy

CHAPTER TEN

Will rushed home, took a quick shower, then bolted out the door. It was already ten minutes past six. He didn't want Carmella walking into The Blue Grotto thinking he'd stood her up. As it happens they both pulled into the restaurant's parking lot at the same time.

Carmella looked really good. She'd left work a little early to get her nails done and go shopping for new shoes. This was not a date, but it was the closest thing to a date she'd been on in quite a while.

Spider was dressed in his regular evening attire. A comfortable pair of Levi's, 32 inch waist, paired with a black T-shirt and Harley-Davidson motorcycle boots. He looked buff. At least Carmella thought so.

The detective held the door for his non date, then pointed to a table with a view of the Intracoastal. No sooner had they sat down when a double masted schooner approached from the South. Will said it was most likely heading up to St. Augustine. He'd heard there was a fleet of Tall Ships assembling there in preparation for a cross Atlantic sailing. They watched in silence as the schooner sailed past and disappeared from view.

When the waitress arrived she suggested several drink specials the restaurant was offering. Carmella raised her arm in the air to cut her off. *"That's okay, we'll have two dirty martinis,"* she announced. Then she looked over at Will and said, *"My treat."*

Conversation was minimal as the two of them sat waiting for their drink order to arrive. Will just smiled and tapped his fingers on the edge of the table. At one point he decided to rearrange the items in the condiment tray. Meanwhile Carmella fussed with her hair and scanned the room, as if she was looking to see if she recognized anyone. The five minutes felt like fifty. When the waitress finally returned with their drinks Will asked her if there were any specials on the dinner menu. Then he turned to Carmella and jokingly said, *"The last thing I wanna do is break the budget, seeing how it's your treat and all."*

The comment seemed to break up the logjam. Carmella giggled and even blushed a little. From that point on everything went much more smoothly. On the waitress suggestion they went with the special of the night. If you ordered one prime rib dinner you got the second one for half off. A really great deal, so they were told. When it came time to refresh their drinks Will opted for a cold beer instead of another martini. He told Carmella, *"that martini was good, but no where near as good as yours was the other night. In case you were wondering why I switched."*

"Now how would you know that," she countered. *"You slept through my martinis."*

Will explained that after waking up to find himself sprawled out on her sofa he couldn't help but notice the half filled martini glass on the side table. *"You must have noticed the glass was empty when you got up,"* the detective stated with a big grin on his face. *"I mean y'all ain't never gonna make detective if you don't pick up on clues like that."*

Carmella laughed at Will's comment, and assured him she was quite happy right where she was, *"thank you very much!"* When dinner arrived they ate in relative silence. Afterwards the mood turned more serious. *"Is there any more news on that suicide,"* Carmella asked? *"I can't believe that kid killed himself. It's such a shame. I feel so bad for his mother. That young man had the whole world in the palm of his hands.*

Spider suggested she probably felt that way because the kid was such a well known figure. The fact he was a local boy made it more interesting. He told her about the medical examiner's report, and the stack of 8X10 glossies he'd sent over. He mentioned they were actually still sitting in a manila envelope in the trunk of his car. He'd forgotten about them with everything that happened during that fiasco at the biker bar that afternoon.

Carmella immediately asked if she could see them. Will hesitated. *"I've got to warn you, Carm. They ain't real pretty… And we just ate."*

She responded by reminding him she'd been around a while. *"I've seen it all, Detective. A victim advocate deals with a lot of shit. We are involved in nearly every death, every rape, every child abuse case that comes down the pike. A few pictures aren't going to send me running for the ladies room. If they did make me sick I'd walk away."*

Spider said okay, then excused himself and ran out to retrieve the photos from his car. When he got back he emptied the manila folder onto the table and shuffled them into a neat two inch pile.

When it came time to sit down Will swung over to Carmella's side of the table. He said it was so they could finger through them together. While going through the pile together their legs touched but neither of them acted as if they realized it.

An eerie silence seemed to hang in the air as the two of them studied the photographs. There was no discussion of what they were looking at. Nor did anyone come over to the table to ask them how everything was or if they needed anything. The waitress seemed to have disappeared. Even the mood music playing in the background fell silent. It felt like it does when you're a little early for church and you're sitting in a pew waiting for the service to start. Hushed whispers and the occasional cough the only sounds. Carmella would pick up a photo, study it for half a minute, then flip it over and move to the next one, all without uttering a word.

When she got to the last photo in the pile Carmella broke the silence. She mumbled something undecipherable, but Will picked up on it. *"What did you say,"* he asked?

"Did you see that" she repeated? This time loud enough so Will could understand her. *"There's something under his left eye brow. I know it's kind of gross because his eyeball is missing, but look. There's a tiny little tattoo on his left eyelid."*

Spider placed his hand on Carmella's knee for support and scooted closer so he could see what she was referring to. Then he picked up his water glass, gulped down what remained, and held it upside down over the photograph. He was hoping to magnify the spot where Carmella thought she saw something. It took a moment but Will eventually spotted it too. A tiny tattoo, right there on the kid's left eyelid.

It looked like some kind of symbol. It was hard to make out because of the blackened skin it was part of. Even the medical examiner had missed it. Upon closer inspection Will could see the tattoo depicted a tiny triangle, and inside the triangle was what appeared to be an eye. He didn't think it looked like a human eye though. It was more like a snake's eye. The triangle had a burst of sun rays around it, as if illuminating the eye that it held. Directly below the triangle were the letters N. O. S. *"What do you make of that,"* Carmella asked?

"I don't make anything of it," Spider responded. *"Lots of rock stars have tattoos these days, even the women. Who knows why he chose that one. I have a few myself."*

He didn't have to say so. Everybody in the police department knew about Will Durance's tattoos. They were infamous. He'd gotten one of them overseas when he was in the army. It depicted an American flag with the inscription, FREEDOM IS NOT FREE. Another tattoo, the more infamous one, he'd gotten while working an undercover assignment as a member of a special state task force investigating criminal motorcycle gang activity. That one depicted a large spider. His namesake. That damn tattoo had saved his ass.

As the story goes the detective had been called out on the carpet by the leader of this badass biker gang he'd infiltrated. One of the gang's members had gotten suspicious about Will and made those suspicions known to the gang's GP. Spider's loyalty had come into question. A very compromising position to be in.

During the interrogation the club GP asked Will how he got the name Spider. Fearing his cover was blown the detective made up some bullshit story about having spent this one weekend with a chick whose husband happened to be of all things a born again Christian evangelist. He told the gang leader the soul saving husband was hardly ever home so he spent the weekend snorting cocaine and fucking the guy's wife's brains out.

Will said he woke up two days later to find this big old spider tattoo splashed across his arm. The crazy bitch he was fucking had called in some tattoo artist friend of hers and had them both done. The bitch had this tattoo artist friend of hers place her spider tattoo so it looked like the fucking thing was crawling right out of her snatch.

The GP was so enthralled with Will's story he forgot all about the serious accusation one of the gang members had made against him. The information Detective Durance gathered from that undercover operation landed the gang president and several gang members in the Florida State Penitentiary. They are all up in Starke, Florida serving very long prison sentences on a second degree murder rap.

Carmella decided to drop the subject but it still bothered her. There was something about that tiny tattoo that didn't feel right. Where it was placed, and what it represented. The stack of photographs had kind of put a damper on the mood. You don't look at something like that then go about your business as usual. The brutal death of a young gifted singer like Jeremy London left you wondering, why? Even if it was by his own hand.

After Carm paid the tab Will escorted her to her car, then made his way across the parking lot to his. He got behind the wheel then sat there awhile looking at the lights twinkling from the long row of hotels that lined the ocean in the distance. Daytona Beach sure was pretty at night, he thought. At least from that vantage point.

Once he was home Spider emptied the manila envelope out on his kitchen table one more time, then fingered through the pile of photos until he found the one he was looking for. He then got up to retrieve a magnifying glass he always carried in his briefcase. As he held the photo up his mentor's words came back to him. *"Things are not always what they seem, Will. They're very seldom what they seem."*

AN AMERICAN IDOL
The Illuminati Conspiracy

CHAPTER ELEVEN

June London could find no peace. Her only child had been taken from her. Stolen by greed. They'd used him for their own narcissistic glory. She knew who they were. God had revealed them to her. Her son was the victim of a ritualistic sacrifice. A sacrifice carried out by people who put the love of money above all else. She'd watched the Super Bowl. She'd seen the half-time show. The satanic symbolism and disgusting subliminal messaging had not escaped her watchful eye. Jeremy was murdered by a morbid collection of acedia freaks incapable of showing remorse for the suffering they cultivate.

He'd been so close to redemption that day on the beach. When Jeremy turned and ran it was the beginning of the end. He didn't realize it then, but he hadn't run from that group of unruly thugs who tried to embarrass him. Nor was he running from the clutches of an overbearing mother who wouldn't stop hounding him about the need to confess his sins and repent. No, her Jeremy had run from God.

June always had good intentions. Wanting her son to get saved was not a bad thing. What she couldn't seem to see was that the problem wasn't the message, it was the method. Much like the ignorant street preacher who unwittingly pushes the very sinners he is trying to save away with his dire warnings of eternal damnation. What June needed to understand is that salvation is a message of love. It's not about spreading guilt and fear. Maybe if she'd just stuck to praying for her only son things might have been different for them both.

After being crucified on the cross for the sins of the world Jesus spent three days in hell atoning for them. Only then was the stone rolled away from his tomb so he could fulfill his mission. So too had June London. But now her atonement was complete. It was time to go on the offensive.

She contacted her son's old employer up in Flagler County hoping to find out how she could reach the company's president and chief executive officer. She learned it wouldn't be too difficult at all. He was already in town. Jon Heller usually spent several months a year wintering in the Daytona Beach area. It was his home away from home.

June knew she wouldn't get an appointment with Jonathan Heller just by asking. Who would want to talk to the grieving mother of a child who took his own life? She'd almost certainly be looking for someone to blame. Instead she would just plow past the half dozen photo journalist camped out on the sidewalk in front of her home and drive up to the motorcycle parts distributor's beachside facility. She arrived nearly an hour before it was scheduled to open.

Jonathan Heller did not get where he was by accident. The Hell on Wheels Motorcycle Parts executive made a habit of arriving for work at least thirty minutes before his employees were scheduled too. What better example to set than that? Heller was midway between his rented Lexus and the employees entrance when June London approached him.

"Excuse me... Mr. Heller... Sir... I'm sorry to intrude... May I have a few minutes of your time... Please, Sir?"

The multimillionaire motorcycle parts supplier fancied himself a man of the people. He took pride in the fact he never forgot where he came from, like so many others do once they've made it to the top. "Yes, certainly, Ma'am," he answered. "What did we do, mess up your order? I can get someone to help you with that. We don't open for another half hour though. Tell you what. Come on in. I'll put on some coffee and you can wait inside."

"Okay...so he seems like a nice guy," June thought to herself. "Maybe I need to approach this from a different angle?" She followed her son's former employer inside, all the while trying to decide her best course of action. When Heller told her she could wait in the employee lobby upstairs she knew her options were limited.

After climbing the stairs to the second floor Heller pointed toward the employee break room and told June he would join her there in a few minutes. He needed to go to his office and check his messages. He started to walk away but then turned and said, *"You know, you look a little familiar to me, Madam... Have we met?"*

"No Sir, we have never met, Mr. Heller. I'm June London," she blurted out. *"Jeremy's Mom."*

"Oh my God... Of course." Heller responded. *"I'm so sorry, Mrs. London. I heard the news. It's terrible. Please, ma'am... If there is anything I can do. Anything at all..."*

Rather than leave the distraught lady standing there all alone in the hallway Heller gently took her arm and escorted her inside the break room. He quickly made a pot of coffee then joined her at one of the tables overlooking the showroom floor.

"It is a tragedy, Mrs. London... The boy had so much to live for. I understand he has a new album coming out after the first of the year. I am sure it will go platinum, just like the others. Especially now!"

June acted as though she didn't hear a word Heller said. *"You know how he died,"* she asked? Without waiting for a response she answered. *"Suicide, Mr. Heller... They are saying my boy went and hung himself. My boy... Supposedly put a noose around his neck and jumped off the end of the Daytona Beach Pier... My boy!""*

Her painful announcement was followed by dead silence. That is until the sound of the elevator doors opening broke it. A moment later Heller's secretary walked past the break room. She was fumbling with the keys in her purse and never noticed them. Heller turned to the obviously upset mother and asked, *"What can I do for you, Mrs. London? Your son was very special to me. I was quite proud of him. Do you need help with funeral expenses?"*

June cut him off mid-sentence. *"My son was murdered, Mr Heller. Do you understand? He was killed... Sacrificed. Those bloodsucking vampires out in California did that to my boy. I know it...and I think you do too!"*

The man rose from his seat, teetered momentarily, then took a step back. *"You're upset, Mrs. London... That's understandable. Did you come here alone? Is there a Mr. London? Perhaps you should let me call someone."*

The distraught mother stood and glanced around the room for a moment, then calmly headed for the door. Heller heard her mutter, *"No, I'm fine."* as she walked out.

Larry London was busy waxing the shafts of his golf clubs when his wife walked in the front door. *"Where have you been,"* he asked. *"We had visitors."* It was true. Three visitors had come to the door after June left that morning. Elliot Prince had told Larry he traveled all the way from Los Angeles to pay his respects. The CEO of Head-Hunter Media Group was accompanied by his attorney, a pencil thin guy in a Brooks Brothers suit named Cecile D'ville, and Richard Tejada, the Lieutenant Governor of Florida.

"They came here to offer their condolences," Larry told his wife. *"When the lieutenant governor saw me waxing my shafts he asked me if I wanted to join them for a round of golf tomorrow morning. Imagine that... We are meeting out at Legends Golf Course."*

June told her husband Elliot Prince had not traveled all the way from California to pay his respects. *"He was in Orlando,"* she huffed. *"Our son was supposed to be on television last night. Jeremy was starring in a live pay per view Christmas special. Read the papers once in a while, Goddamn it!"*

With that she stormed off. As soon as June disappeared around the corner her husband mocked her. *"Read the papers once in a while... Ba Fungool, Bitch!"*

Jeremy's funeral was scheduled to be held the following Thursday afternoon. June's pastor and members of his staff were planning the arrangements. Jeremy would be remembered in a private ceremony, then buried at an undisclosed location. June didn't want her son's death to be a mockery. She had read all about the shenanigans that happen in places like Jim Morrison's burial site. Whiskey bottles and women's panties strewn all over the former singer's headstone like the party never ended. That door was permanently closed.

In her mourning June had spoken with God. They had a very special relationship, she and Him. June believed it was God who revealed the truth about Jeremy's death to her. Her son did not kill himself. Not that he wouldn't have eventually. Few who live that lifestyle survive very long to talk about it. The list goes on and on.

She'd been shown a vision. A dream of sorts. It was the night before she got the terrible news. The night before the detective and that victim advocate lady showed up at her door. Her son was in trouble. Jeremy's performance at the Super Bowl last year had convinced her of that. She was happy he'd been able to fulfill his dream but sorry about the path he'd chosen. Better to be a less successful Christian singer, she'd thought. At least he'd still be alive.

In her dream her son had been seduced by a demoness. The snake eyed succubus was ultra sexy, but in a very demented and disturbing way. She wore a bustier that exposed her breasts. Her nipples were large and very erect. When Jeremy went to suckle them they changed shape. June realized they weren't really nipples at all. They were tiny penises.

As Jeremy suckled on them the succubus's penis/nipples ejaculated a nasty liquid into her son's mouth. A slimy pellucid liquid. Rather than swallow it Jeremy seemed to absorb the liquid as it coated his throat. He immediately went into violent convulsions. June watched in horror as the spasms shook her baby boy senseless. They lasted for what seemed like an eternity. When they finally subsided the curvaceous demoness lifted Jeremy high above her head and began moaning a strange repetitious chant. "Novus Ordo Seclorum. Novus Ordo Seclorum. Novus Ordo Seclorum.

Suddenly and without warning the evil being let go of her son, but instead of plunging to the ground Jeremy levitated in the air above the demonic woman's head. Then he started spinning. The faster the demoness chanted her chant the faster the boy spun.

Then as suddenly as it had started the spinning stopped. The evil succubus reached up and drew Jeremy's body down toward her, stopping when his face was inches from hers. Something resembling a tongue came out of the demonic's mouth. A long, leathery organ that gave off a putrid stench. It wrapped itself around the young singer's throat. When the length of it was completely extended the tongue like organ contracted.

The violent spasmodic movement forced Jeremy's eyeballs to pop from their sockets. When the demonic saw this she laughed, then loosened her grip. Her tongue like organ recoiled back down her throat. The evil succubus then turned to June and in a gravely hoarse voice bragged, "I just strangled your baby right before his very eyes..."

When June woke from her dream she was covered in sweat. The vision had been so horrifyingly real she attempted to contact her son

to warn him about what she'd seen but he wasn't answering his cell phone. She knew Jeremy was in Florida. Local television news anchors had been talking about his live pay per view Christmas special for days. The front page of the local newspaper ran a headline that read, AN AMERICAN IDOL COMES HOME FOR THE HOLIDAYS. He came home all right... In a box!

AN AMERICAN IDOL
The Illuminati Conspiracy

CHAPTER TWELVE

Stanton Price Jr, with the help of hand selected cohorts, had made his mark on the world. A monumental feat considering his less than privileged upbringing. Stanton wasn't a Rothschild or a Rockefeller. His bloodlines couldn't be traced to the Merovingian Kings of Europe. Stanton was chosen to lead the Illuminati precisely because he wasn't a public figure. Outside the California commercial real estate market Stanton Price Jr, was relatively unknown.

Most of the Illuminati's business is carried out from the organizations headquarters outside La Jolla, California. They have transformed America's 'left coast' into its core of operations. The Illuminati have their stamp of approval on everything from the LA music scene to the Hollywood film industry. From the television studios to the wineries of Napa Valley. They even control the tech industry that makes up the Silicon Valley.

The California agriculture consortium, itself a twenty-billion dollar a year industry, is under Illuminati control too. The Central Valley of California has some of the most fertile farming soil in the world. At nearly twenty-five thousand acres it can produce enough to feed the entire population of the earth. At least it will once the final plan is enacted.

Illuminati income isn't limited to those so called 'legal' enterprises either. They have their hands on everything from illegal narcotics to the thriving porn industry. From international money laundering to wholesale arms dealing. The Illuminati's association with Columbian drug cartels and Jihadi terrorists runs blood deep too. There is no limit to the secret society's reach.

The truth is the term 'secret society' is in reality a misnomer. Nearly everyone in the entertainment industry is aware of its existence. Anyone remotely associated with Hollywood understands how it all works. There is not one single actor, film director, music publisher, or movie producer who doesn't understand that if they want to survive they need to bow down in reverence. Amazingly not one of them know for certain who they are actually bowing too...

Almost no one asks questions. The few that do end up overdosing on heroin or crack. Or they are institutionalized after suffering mental breakdowns. Some are arrested and convicted of crimes they swear on their mother's grave they did not commit. Some simply disappear. The lucky ones are castigated as has beens with a vendetta against the very industry that once supported them. And some end up just like Jeremy Tobias London.

Yes, Stanton Price, Jr. has made his mark on the world, but he has plenty of accomplices. Take Elliot Prince for instance. He is the preeminent music producer in the industry. His collection of world famous artists includes the biggest names in rock, rap, and pop. He decides what America, and therefore the world, listens too.

Then there is the Bathgate twins. They run Hollywood. Those two boys have produced the most successful blockbuster films of the last two decades. Together they control who sees what. They determine who in the film industry works and who doesn't. Even the few 'independents' who occasionally slip through the cracks only do so because a Bathgate boy allowed it.

Talia Barber rules the television industry. She, along with her massive web of underlings, decides what America watches on a nightly basis. Without her seal of approval a show can't even get on the air, much less draw an audience. Talia has the power to make a huge star out of a complete unknown virtually overnight. She can relegate someone who falls out of line to the dung heap just as quickly. Any number of once recognizable faces can attest to that.

None of which is bad in and of itself. After all someone has to be in charge. It has been said many are called but few are chosen, and that is true. And it is Stanton Price, Jr. who does the choosing these days. The Elliot Prince's and the Bathgate's, even the Talia Barber's of the world, are a necessary evil. What would society become without individuals like them? Individuals who possess the foresight and purpose to get things done. The problem isn't that power is placed in the hands of the few. It is what the few choose to do with that power.

When the object of the game is mind control. When the freedom to choose one's own path is unwittingly altered by outside forces, that's when it becomes a problem. The sad part is we refuse to see what our own eyes try to show us. God is not a concept. I would suggest the idea that he is, is itself a concept.

Illuminati interest in the USA isn't limited to the West Coast. Several members of the Congressional Oversight Committee report directly to Stanton Price, Jr. He also has eyes and ears on the Ways and Means Committee, the Appropriations Committee, and the Office of Inspector General.

Several members of the National Banking Commission are pawns of the Illuminati also, as is the National Director of the Office of Foreign Relations. It is an impressive array, one that features the finest minds in America, and all dedicated to one cause.

The Illuminati's European headquarters is located outside Brussels, Belgium. Like its western counterpart society membership consists of the best and brightest the European continent has to offer. They come from the arts, science and industry, government, the banking industry, even European royalty.

None see their involvement as counter productive. The centuries old society is simply following the law of nature. The strong survive and the weak perish. Everything is as it should be.

Stanton Price, Jr. does not normally get involved in triviality. As head of the Council of Thirteen he oversees the big picture. His job is to keep everyone focused. But in an unexplainable and yet undeniable moment of weakness Stanton set off a sequence of events that will sadly alter the course of human history.

AN AMERICAN IDOL
The Illuminati Conspiracy

BOOK TWO

CHAPTER THIRTEEN

Felecia Emmons met Jeremy London while performing her duties as a sound mixer on the American Idol television show once it returned to its Hollywood, California setting. A chance meeting lead to the two of them becoming very close. They both agree it wasn't a sexual thing, though they did have sex. It was more a bonding of souls.

Felecia was very spiritual, just not in a typical Christian way. She didn't believe in heaven or hell. Nor did she buy into the notion that there would be a reconciliation with, or resurrection of, the physical body in the afterlife. Felecia believed that when a human being is conceived a spiritual being is also born. This spiritual being resides in the physical body of its hosts until its host can no longer provide it shelter. It then ascends to its higher calling.

She often compared it to being like a caterpillar. When a caterpillar is conceived it eventually transforms itself into something other than what it was. When the original caterpillar body is no longer able to provide its spiritual self shelter the spiritual self is free to ascend to its higher calling. In this case a butterfly. So it is with us.

It was this spiritualism that attracted Felecia to Jeremy in the first place. She felt as if their spirits were entwined. She was in the studio one day manipulating reverbs and delays on one of the contestant's tracks when she first felt him. Jeremy was wandering around the studio killing time waiting for his number to be called when he happened to walk by Felecia's work station. When he did the hair on the back of Felecia's neck stood up. Not only that, the audio mixing machine she was using suddenly quit working. Someone else may have suspected the two events were the result of an electrical malfunction or some sort. A mechanical failure. But not Felecia. She immediately opened the studio door and upon seeing Jeremy standing there, asked him to come in.

The two of them became kindred spirits. Two peas in a pod as it were. Felecia very likely had something to do with Jeremy London winning the competition. She employed several innovative techniques to improve the quality and crispness of his voice, as well as his guitar. She reconfigured her computer to mimic the eight track effects that Dave Stewart employed to produce the soundtrack for the Eurythmics chart topping Sweet Dreams LP. No one could call it cheating. It was her job to make everyone in the competition sound as good as she possibly could, and that is exactly what she did.

Felecia left the American Idol gig shortly after Jeremy signed with Head-Hunter Records. He asked her to move in with him and she accepted. It would have been tempting for him to fall under the intoxicating spell of stardom. Felecia understood that once someone is exposed to the excesses of life in the spotlight it can be difficult to resist the notion that it is somehow deserved. As if one was divinely appointed to the post. The idea that someone might have simply been in the right place at the right time, or that they were the recipient of another's good will, becomes fodder for the foolish. Felecia truly thought she could help keep him centered.

She made sure Jeremy retained his youthful exuberance, and that he show appreciation for his good fortune. She insisted that her very talented singer/boyfriend give credit where credit was due. When Felecia learned Jeremy had alienated himself from his family she set out to repair the relationship.

Unbeknownst to him Felecia had spoken to Jeremy's mother on the telephone. This happened on two separate occasions. The first was shortly after he signed his first record deal. A huge celebration was planned to commemorate the event and Felecia thought Jeremy's parents should be there. His mother told her she would consider attending but only if her son himself invited her... It would have to be a personal invitation, from him and him alone.

That was not going to happen. And the reason he gave was this. His mother would verbalize her displeasure with Felecia's spiritualist beliefs. His bible thumping martinet of a mother would embarrass him with her long drawn out Christian disquisition. Besides, she'd never once apologized for the way she treated him following that humiliating baptism fiasco that day at the beach when he was a kid. It may have been a long time ago, but the effects of it still lingered.

The second time the two women spoke was the day before Felecia disappeared. She'd called Mrs. London to ask her if she would consider coming out to California. Felecia seemed frantic, as if she knew something terrible was going to happen. But she never let on what it was. June dismissed her request, saying she would need to pray about it because she was not one to make decisions without seeking out the Lord's will first.

She never heard from Felecia after that. June didn't know what happened. She assumed Jeremy and the girl had a squabble of some sort. Her first impression of the young sound technician had been quite positive. She'd secretly wished they might get together but that would require them to marry. There would be no living in sin. Not if they wanted Mom's approval.

She had no idea the two of them were already living together. She also had no idea what happened to her either. She just disappeared. Jeremy was on the road finishing up a three month tour of the midwest. He only had two more shows scheduled. One at Chaifetz Arena in St Louis, Missouri and one at the Kauffman Performing Arts Center in Kansas City. Then he would be home.

The two of them talked often when they were apart. Jeremy would call Felecia half a dozen times a day. Then a few days before his tour was coming to an end she just stopped answering her cell phone. Jeremy didn't know why. When he got back to Los Angeles he honestly expected to discover she had somehow managed to lose it. Instead he found she'd up and left him. Her clothes and personal effects were gone. The house was neat as a pin. There wasn't a single sign she'd ever been there. No note. Nothing. Not so much as a hint about what might have caused her to vanish into thin air.

Jeremy called everyone he could think of trying to find her. Nobody knew where Felecia was. No one had seen her in days. As far as he knew she had no family. She'd told him she never knew her father and that her mom had died of cancer when she was sixteen. He was all she had, and Jeremy felt the same way about her. He couldn't believe she just up and left him like that, but it appeared she had.

A part of her remained with him. Felecia had taught Jeremy her secret to happiness. What kept her grounded and in touch with her true self. He tried to employ it as a way of making sense of what happened. It was a simple equation. Felecia referred to it as Ying and Yang. If there is a before, there has to be an after. If there is a

high, then there has to be a low. When you see something as beautiful, something else becomes ugly. Work hard, but take time to step back. You are a vessel, fill your emptiness with what you will. Things will come, things will go... Let them." All Felecia Emmons euphemisms. It is how he survived...

AN AMERICAN IDOL
The Illuminati Conspiracy

CHAPTER FOURTEEN

Elliot Prince wasn't a golfer but he was a shrewd business man. If the lieutenant governor wanted to play a round so be it. As for Cecile D'Ville, he would do as he was told. The attorney didn't particularly like the game but he was a pretty decent player. When they arrived at Legends Clubhouse D'Ville offered to team up with Larry London.

It was quite warm out considering it was almost New Year's Day. Temperatures were in the low 70's. Larry had arrived at the golf course first so he went ahead and reserved two golf carts. When the clubhouse manager learned the lieutenant governor was going to be gracing his greens that day he waived the fee.

As the host Larry insisted his illustrious guest tee off first. The portly politician removed a custom made Precision X driver from his bag and took a couple practice swings. Then he swaggered over and placed his ball on the tee.

Richard Tejada knew his away around a golf course. He was a member of the very exclusive Pelican Bay Golf Club over in Naples. Before serving as lieutenant governor Tejada had represented the twenty-third district in the state legislature. If there was one thing the politician could point to that helped him get elected it was golf. He'd made many friends on the links, and made many deals.

One of those friends was an elderly black man named Tazmania Bones. Taz was a well known recording artist who settled in Naples after deciding to retire from the music industry. He has won several Grammy Awards over the years, and had a slew of hit records. A native of Detroit, Taz was a founding member of the popular soul group The Accusers. The band split up back in the late seventies. Taz Bones later became a very successful record producer after signing an exclusive deal with Head-Hunter Records. It was Taz Bones who introduced Tejada to Elliot Prince.

In those days Prince was just getting started in the music business. He had serious financial backing and was recruiting talent for the new record label. Taz Bones was one of his first acquisitions. Bones liked to tell all his black brothers back in Detroit that Prince could sweet talk his way through a gauntlet of club wielding racist white policemen at an inner city race riot. Spend five minutes with Elliot Prince and he'll have you eating out of his hand.

Richard Tejada was no exception. Both men could help each other. Tejada needed national exposure to get where he was going. Being seen in the company of a super successful recording artist like Taz Bones would give the up and coming politician instant credibility. Elliot Prince needed to show he could pocket young upstarts and groom them to carry out the interests of the organization. Elliot had the unique ability to spot susceptible, yet otherwise very competent people and use them for his own ends.

The pudgy politician standing in the tee box was being primed for a run at the White House. By the time he was ready to make the move America's Latino population would be close to a hundred million strong. Sixty percent of them eligible to vote. Just as importantly the majority of them would live in states with the most electoral college votes. If the timing was right Tejada would be President of the United States when Stanton Price, Jr. was ready to make his move.

It was Stanton who interrupted the lieutenant governor just as he was taking his swing. The politician's ball tailed off to the right and bounced across the adjacent parking lot, causing him to react in a true fit of anger.

Stanton Price had ordered his chauffeur to pull his limo right up to the fairway. When the rear door opened and Stanton stepped out of the automobile Tejada looked over in disbelief. He apologized for his tirade then rushed over to greet him. Unfortunately Elliott Prince beat him to the punch. Stanton wrapped his arms around his underling and kissed him on both cheeks. Cecile D'ville and Larry London remained in their golf carts watching the entire scene unfold. Neither man knew who the hell Stanton Price, Jr was.

Stanton told his colleagues that he decided to come to Florida because he needed to get away for a while. Take a little vacation. It was just that simple. A visit to the Sunshine State was in order. Besides, it would allow him an opportunity to touch base with some old friends. Stanton mentioned he might stick around and attend the Jeremy London funeral.

Truth be known he'd promised Felecia Emmons he would. It was her dying wish. She'd pleaded with Stanton to let her ashes be buried with Jeremy. So why not grant the small favor. After all the misguided spiritualist had made the ultimate sacrifice, had she not? Not without a struggle mind you, but still... An offering is an offering.

He really liked the young woman. If only she'd gone along with the program. Stanton Price saw her failure as his failure. In the end he realized it would be best if she were no longer in the picture. When Elliot Prince suggested sacrificing her for the cause Stanton was quick to agree.

He'd brought with him a vial containing a portion of Felecia Emmons remains. Her reproductive organs actually, if his orders had been carried out properly. The Grand Pindar of the Draco would be certain that vial made its way into the dead singer's casket. After all, "what God hath joined together..."

Cecile D'ville was happy to yield his spot on the card to Stanton. The accommodating lawyer became official scorekeeper for the remainder of the afternoon. The Grand Pindar feigned surprise when introduced to Larry London, offering his heartfelt condolences at Jeremy's passing. The not so remorseful father eagerly shook Stanton Price's hand, and suggested they pair up.

The team of Lieutenant Governor Tejada and Elliot Prince won the round. Larry London kept the score close, finishing just one stroke behind the Florida politician at one under par.

Jeremy's dad had no way of knowing the men he'd spent the day golfing with were Illuminati. Nor did he have any idea they were directly responsible for his son's death. "What the Lord giveth, the Lord taketh away..."

Larry London was easily impressed, and these were powerful men. When Elliot Prince jumped out of his golf cart and sprinted over to Stanton Price's limousine it was as if the man was some kind of God. Larry thought he must be in the presence of royalty. He was more than a little surprised to discover Stanton was just a California real estate developer, albeit a very successful one. If someone as wealthy and successful as Elliot Prince was displaying reverential obeisance to the likes of him Larry figured he must have chosen the wrong profession to be in.

Stanton Price, Jr. took Larry aside and told him he didn't know his son personally but that he understood Jeremy was an extremely talented musician. He offered to help with the funeral expenses, and asked for permission to attend the service. Needless to say Larry London grinned from ear to ear.

This was not happening. He was a small time insurance salesman. A hack who earned forty-five thousand dollars a year peddling life insurance policies to retired firefighters from New Jersey, and here he was in the company of the most successful record producer in America, a future president of the United States, and a billionaire real estate developer from California. All because his son tried out for American Idol.

Larry provided his new friends with the details of Jeremy's funeral. His son would be buried the following Thursday afternoon. A service was being held at the Pentecostal Assembly Church in New Smyrna Beach. Larry explained his wife was hoping to keep the funeral private, with only relatives and close friends of the family attending. They'd decided to have the funeral at the church, rather than attempt a viewing at a funeral home. Mrs. London feared a mockery would be made if details were publicized.

Stanton Price, Jr's personal involvement in this type of thing was highly unusual. Normally there would be five layers of protection around him. The Grand Pindar didn't like getting his hands dirty. Far be it from him to be caught in a national scandal.

It's not that he didn't know lives were being sacrificed for the cause. On the contrary it happened quite frequently. As Grand Pindar of the Draco the man understood the big picture. It should be considered an honor to give one's life for the greater good. Once the dust settled, once he'd fulfilled his destiny, over eighty-five percent of the human race would have that honor.

The plan was in motion. Stanton was a man of his word. He'd attend the funeral, but remain in the background, which is how it should be. He'd be there to pay his respects as the friend of a friend. No one would know him or what he was really up to. When the time came Stanton would approach the casket, fulfill his obligation, and slip out.

It wasn't like Stanton Price to acquiesce to the dying wishes of a sacrificial lamb. Felecia Emmons had been an exception. Stanton himself had partaken in her bloodletting. Had he not looked into her eyes as they went lifeless or allowed her the chance to speak prior to it might have been different. Who's to say?

But she had become a danger. She'd interfered with the plan. A plot that had been devised by the greatest minds in human history. To allow her to destroy the work of generations would be comparable to the destruction of mankind for religious reasons. A potential outcome they were desperately trying to prevent.

When they were finished golfing Elliot suggested the five of them go back to the clubhouse for drinks. As much as Larry wanted to he declined. He was scheduled to give a life insurance seminar to a group of retired condo owners at four o'clock. Not wanting to sound working class he made up a story about needing to meet his wife at the church to finalize his son's funeral arrangements. Truth is he'd never stepped foot in that church in his life. After agreeing to meet the others for breakfast the next morning Larry headed out.

AN AMERICAN IDOL
The Illuminati Conspiracy

CHAPTER FIFTEEN

Dinner that night consisted of leftover pepperoni pizza. If you asked Larry he'd have told you the conversation he and his wife shared over dinner was colder than the beer he washed the pizza down with. June was not a happy camper. She'd urged her husband not to go on his golf outing with that pack of heathens but he'd ignored her. Had she been home when they stopped by the day before he definitely would not have. Of that she was certain.

June London had no doubt Elliot Prince had something to do with her son's death. He was evil. A devil in a fancy suit. She didn't care if he was one of the most influential men in the recording industry. Or that he employed some of the biggest names in the music business. He was behind all that nonsense at the Super Bowl. All those encrypted messages and pagan symbolism that was flashing across everyone's television screens that day was his doing. The man was an abomination to Almighty God.

The image of a football stadium packed with fans diving over one another in a desperate attempt to gather as many neon colored bank notes as humanly possible would be ingrained in her conscience for the rest of her life. June knew all that insanity was an Elliot Prince inspiration.

Many in the crowd had gone into an actual state of frenzy. A number of people were seriously injured in the affair. They could have been killed... And all for the love of money. Prince had made her son very rich, that much is true... But at what cost?

Larry couldn't understand his wife's animosity. These men had come to Florida to show their respects. To offer their condolences for the loss of their son. June was directing her grief and anger towards them as though they'd killed him. Larry had to remind her their son had committed suicide. He'd hung himself. *"Those men did not kill Jeremy, Honey.... If anybody is responsible it's us."*

Later that night June was in her son's bedroom, well what used to be his bedroom, taking down some of the personal effects still hanging on his walls. She'd left her son's room pretty much the way it was thinking he was just going through a rebellious stage and he'd come back when he discovered how cold the world could be. The thought he might actually make it all the way to the top of the music industry never entered her mind. He was just a kid from New Smyrna Beach. A self taught guitarist who played for spare change. His chances of making it to the big time were a billion to one.

June took down the last remaining remnant hanging on her son's wall. A photograph she'd taken of him when he was just eleven years old. Ironically he was holding a toy plastic guitar to his chest and he had a big smile on his face. That smile might have hinted at things to come. How June longed for those days. She would definitely do things differently.

For one thing she'd be more involved in her son's life. She would consider his hopes and aspirations, and discuss them with him. She would encourage him to follow his hopes and dreams. She questioned whether the time she'd spent studying the bible and in meditative prayer might have been better spent being a mother.

June had yet another disturbing dream that night. This time she was visited by an angelic figure who called himself Twilight. In a Delphic sort of way Twilight appeared to be manlike. He took the broken hearted woman on a journey. They visited three separate locations, the first being an old abandoned warehouse with faded brick walls. Inside was a large dust covered wooden floor anchored by a long row of windows on the far end. Several of its panes had been shattered by vandals. The evidence lay in the shards of broken glass and rocks that lay scattered around them.

The frightened woman was about to ask the angel where they were when a group of people suddenly appeared at the far end of the cavernous room. All of them wearing black hooded robes. They emptied out of a freight elevator and snaked their way towards the center of the room. Once there they formed a semicircle.

Several more hooded strangers appeared from the shadows. They were pushing what appeared to be some type of examination table towards the center of the room. Horrifically June saw that the table was occupied. A young woman lie spread eagle on it, her feet belted to stirrups on one end and her wrists bound by leather straps on the other. June looked at the angel questioningly but Twilight didn't speak. Instead he pointed to a tall figure who'd just stepped out of the shadows and was making his way towards the table.

Unlike the others gathered there this person was dressed in a finely tailored suit and tie. June went to step towards him but her progress was impeded by Twilight. The angel silently spoke comfort to her, letting her know the vision she was seeing was of the past. He told her what was... was, and that her dream was meant to provide clarity and offer her exoneration from guilt.

Somehow June knew the young woman on the table was Felecia, the girl her son had befriended. She'd spoken to her on the phone a few times but they'd never met. The young woman had seemed upset the last time they talked. As the man in the tailored suit made his way to the center of the room June saw a look of familiarity in Felecia's eyes. It was obvious she knew this guy.

A unified chant welled up from within the black hooded assemblage, as if they were paying homage to him... June had no way of knowing the man in the tailored suit was Stanton Price, Jr. Grand Pindar of the Draco. Her ears filled with the repetitive incantation as it reverberated off the faded brick walls. *"Novus Ordo Seclorum, Novus Ordo Seclorum, Novus Ordo Seclorem."*

Stanton stood directly over the trembling sound engineer and smiled down at her as he brushed a loose strand of hair from her face. Then someone from the semicircle stepped forward. Someone that June London recognized. It was Elliot Prince. The man who'd signed her son to a multimillion dollar record contract. He bowed in reverence to the man in the tailored suit then made his way to the end of the examination table.

June wanted to scream but she found she wasn't able to. It wouldn't have done any good anyway. What was...Was!

Elliot Prince removed his robe and prepared to mount the terrified young woman strapped to the table. As he did Stanton Price leaned forward and in a comforting voice thanked her for being there. He suggested that as of today Felecia Emmons life now had meaning. He told the woman that her sacrifice would help bring mankind one step closer to fulfilling its destiny.

In a strange way Stanton's words did bring some degree of comfort. Felecia had always believed that one's life cycle was predetermined. She referred to it as Kismet. Perhaps this was hers. In a kittenish, almost reconciliatory voice she asked Stanton if he would please allow Jeremy and her to be reunited in the afterlife.

And how could the man refuse the sweet child's last request? The Grand Pindar promised that he would.

On Stanton, Jr's direction Elliot Prince proceeded to have his way with the powerless oblation beneath him. As the middle aged sadist roughly fondled and groped her Felecia closed her eyes and forced herself to think happy thoughts. When the famous record producer felt himself nearing completion of his task he motioned for Stanton to hand him the accouterment he would need to fulfill his endeavor.

The Grand Pindar reached inside his suit coat and pulled out a centuries old solid gold sheath. He admired the antiquity for a moment before handing it to his overzealous ancillary so he could proceed. At the moment of his climax the masochist slammed the razor sharp dagger deep into Felecia Emmons chest.

Blood gushed from the wound, spurting in rhythmic cadence to the sacrificial lamb's last remaining heartbeats. The sadistic henchman then sliced out a six inch square in the woman's chest and removed her still beating heart. He handed it to his Pindar, who held up the clump of throbbing bloody muscle for those standing in the semicircle to see.

June was nauseous. Her dream was so real, and yet so very surreal. No one could be that depraved. No one could possibly profligate in such debauchery...could they? Certainly not in this day and age. I mean, God forbid!

Twilight touched June London's fingertips and she was immediately transcended to yet another domain. A cool breeze was blowing and there was saltiness in the air. The distraught woman found herself standing on a long wooden plank pier. It stretched out over the water and into the darkness. Turning to look back at the angelic figure who'd brought her there June saw several men approaching from the opposite end.

The men appeared to be half carrying, half dragging someone with them. They walked right past her as though she weren't even there.

Without saying so June understood that this too was, what was. She was witnessing a past event, and nothing she could do or say could alter what she was about to see.

When the men got to the end of the pier one of them placed a thick rope around the neck of the person they had forced to accompany them. It was then June realized the poor soul was just a boy, and that he was naked as the wind. Up to that point the identity of the unfortunate had escaped her. It wasn't until the boy was hoisted high above the pier that it hit home. June looked into her son's eyes.

Jeremy was weeping uncontrollably. Held in limbo above the railing of the pier for what seemed like an eternity the trembling youngster let out a desperate cry for help. Unfortunately his plea was lost in the roar of the surf below. June watched as her son's body rose up and over the end of the pier, then dropped from sight.

Before she could let out a scream her anguish was abated. Once again she found herself someplace else. She was now standing in some sort of prison compound. Not a prison in the common sense. She wasn't in a cell, or surrounded by thick walls. It was a prison in that June was somehow aware her freedoms were denied her.

She was standing on a grassy knoll with long lines of people filing past her. Thousands of people. They appeared to be making their way towards a large cement block building up ahead in the distance. Looking up June realized the entire compound was sealed under some sort of transparent dome. She had to look really hard to even see it was there.

Before long a strange looking vehicle approached. Akin to one of those three wheeled motorcycles you see these days. The kind with two wheels in the front and one in the back. This one had a darkly tinted glass roof. As it got closer a voice came from the vehicle, commanding her to get back in line. Somewhat confused, June hesitated. Suddenly a sharp taser like bolt shot out from beneath the vehicle. The ensuing jolt had June on her feet and moving in less than a heartbeat.

The distraught woman was suddenly aware she had lost her escort. Twilight was nowhere to be found. As June fell in line others lined up behind her. Soon there were as many people behind June as there was ahead of her. Looking beyond them she saw there were other lines of people. Long lines, all heading towards similar cement block buildings. June could see the buildings lined the entire perimeter of the enclave. No one in the lines spoke. Not a soul.

Eventually June made it to the entrance of the building. Two tall men in grey jumpsuits stood in the doorway, each holding some type of scanner in their hands. As each person approached one of the men would hold his scanner up to their face. When they did one of two doors would slide open behind them. Most of the people in line were directed through the door on the right. About a quarter of them were directed toward the door on the left.

When it was June's turn she stepped forward cautiously. As the man raised his scanner June realized he wasn't real. I mean he wasn't human. He was a machine. A facsimile of a human being. He appeared to be made out of some type of carbon alloy. He... It... pointed the laser directly into June's eyes. A bright flash blinded her momentarily and a second later the door on the left slid open.

That frightened her. She'd have preferred to join the majority taking the door on the right. June followed the corridor down a long hallway. Suddenly she heard a familiar voice welcoming those fortunate enough to be selected to join him. Turning a corner the hallway emptied into an enormous room.

When the room was filled to capacity a wall slid closed behind them, effectively sealing them in. The lights dimmed and the walls seemed to come alive as the face of a man appeared on them. Someone June recognized from earlier in her dream. It was the same man who'd been worshiped by the throng in the warehouse. The man responsible for Felecia Emmons horrendous death. His face now surrounded her on all four sides.

"Welcome friends," spoke the murderous lunatic to his incarcerated audience. *"Some of you may know me. Some of you may not. In either case I must commend each one of you. You survived the war. The war to end all wars, as it were."*

It's a shame really," he continued. *"All that fighting over such a silly issue. How many people have died in the name of religion over the centuries? Any guesses people? Is it millions? Hundreds of millions? Hardly... The truth is four and a half billion of you were sacrificed in the last war alone."*

"Ah, but that still leaves too many doesn't it. Over three billion are still with us. But the world cannot support those numbers. It never could. That is why you are all here. You nice folks are going to help the world to survive…"

With that all four walls went blank. A moment later the wall on the far end of the room slid open and people began exiting through it. The contingent, numbering close to a thousand souls, made their way down another long corridor. One had the feeling of being herded through the lines of a Disney World attraction on a busy summer day. No one panicked. They all went along like lambs to a slaughter.

The long corridor narrowed before emptying into another large open space. This time when the wall closed behind them there was only silence. With everyone accounted for the wall they faced slowly rolled up into itself. As it ascended toward the ceiling the wall behind them started creeping forward, forcing people onward. Those in the front were greeted by the horrifying realization there was nowhere to run. They found themselves looking straight down into the depths of a dark bottomless pit.

June, who'd been in the middle of the pack, was eventually forced towards the edge too. She was helped along by the hundreds of panicking souls behind her. Just before dropping into the abyss June felt someone take her hand. Next thing she knew she was back in her bed.

AN AMERICAN IDOL
The Illuminati Conspiracy
CHAPTER SIXTEEN

NOS... The tiny tattooed letters were clear as day under Spider's magnifying glass, as was the reptilian eye tattooed on Jeremy London's left eyelid. Carmella Henson had noticed what both he and the medical examiner had originally missed. It was camouflaged by his blackened skin and therefore very hard to see, but still...

Will opened his laptop and began keying in Jeremy London's name. Wikipedia classified the recent suicide victim as an American singer/song writer/American Idol. The online encyclopedia claimed Jeremy London was one of the most prominent mainstream rock&roll recording artists in the music industry today.

According to Wikipedia Jeremy London's first three albums had all gone multi-platinum and he'd won four Grammy Awards. The online encyclopedia also mentioned the singer's overtly spectacular Super

Bowl performance and highlighted Billboard Magazine's claim that Jeremy London singlehandedly saved American rock and roll. It said the talented musician was on course to become one of the most influential rock guitarist of all time, joining such luminaries as Pete Townsend, Jimmy Page, and Jimi Hendrix. That is until his life was cut short.

That's the thing... His life was cut short. Why? Suicide didn't make sense. Regardless of his not so happy childhood the fact is the young man was wildly successful. He had no known history of manic depression. He never displayed any type of pathological psychosis or mental illness. He had no history of drug addiction. His strained relationship with his parents aside Jeremy London was quite normal.

People who are suicidal generally give out warning signs. Obvious calls for help. They find ways to tell others they are in pain. Rarely does someone take his own life on a whim. It is truly a final act of desperation.

Fame, fortune, and glory are not the seeds of despair. Jeremy London was on a golden gondola ride to the top of the mountain. The view from there must be spectacular. It's true that what goes up must come down but the singer's future was set. The only way his life could be adversely affected at this stage would be if someone were to upset the apple cart. And who would want to?

The detective's dinner date with Carmella hadn't gone quite the way he hoped. The head of the police department's victim advocate office was quite shaken when she left the parking lot that evening. Spider questioned his decision to show her the photographs Dr. Rupert had sent him. Perhaps it was a mistake to even mention them to her. He picked up the photos, finger patted them into a neat pile, then slid them back inside the manila envelope. Then his phone rang.

It was Carmella. She wanted to thank Will for dinner and apologize for running off the way she did. Then she admitted the real reason she was calling. Carmella had discovered some information she found very interesting. An article about Jeremy London had been published in Rolling Stone magazine several months before the popular singer's death. Buried in the article was a short paragraph mentioning Jeremy London's unhappiness with his record label and its CEO, Elliot Prince. In response to a question he was asked about the unusual lyrics of a song on his latest album Jeremy was quoted as saying, *"The Prince chooses all my material now. I just sing what I'm told to sing and cash the fucking checks."*

So all was not well in Tinsel Town after all. Any songwriter will tell you he wants to sing his own lyrics, even those without the talent to pull it off. But Jeremy had the talent, so why not let him?

One other line in that Rolling Stone article jumped out at Carmella as she read it. Jeremy had mentioned a girl. It was nondescript, but it hung there like a piece of forbidden fruit. The writer had included the quote in his article but it appeared he did not catch its implication. The sentence read, *"It hasn't been the same without my girlfriend. She really opened my eyes."*

"What do you make of that," Carmella asked Spider? *"Did you know that Jeremy London had a girlfriend? What happened? Where is she? Opened his eyes to what?"*

Will told her not to get too excited. It was just a magazine article, and that the quotes were really noncommittal. Taken out of context it was easy to read into a comment whatever one wanted. Secretly though his juices were flowing. Spider felt himself begin salivating at the information Carmella had fed him.

Thing is it was a closed case. The medical examiner had deemed Jeremy London's death a suicide. Period. End of story. Will knew he would be treading on thin ice. He knew his captain wouldn't support any effort to commit time and resources to reopen a closed case. Not unless Will could show positive proof there was much more to the story than meets the eye. For now he would have to bide his time and work the case incognito, and use his own funds to do so. At least until he had something more substantial than a hunch to offer his superiors.

Next morning Will telephoned June London. He told her he was calling to see how she was doing, and to remind her of the services available through the victim advocates office. He even offered to have Carmella Henson contact her. Before hanging up the detective casually asked June if her son ever mentioned having a girlfriend? There was dead silence on the other end of the line. Will thought perhaps the distraught mother had hung up on him. But then came a response he never expected.

"Yes, Felecia Emmons," she replied. *"My son was in love with her, Detective. Jeremy was heartbroken when she left. He'd been on tour in support of his latest album. He only had a few more concert dates left, then he would have been back in L.A. I've spoken with her several times. She seemed like a good person, though a little flaky… But she did not know God."*

There was an extremely uncomfortable moment of silence before June continued. *"Jeremy wrote to me about her. He wanted us to fly out there to meet her but he was adamant I not bring up God. I was going to anyway. The only way to the Father is through the Son, Detective. It was my sacred obligation to share the..."*

It must have suddenly dawned on her that the detective's line of questioning could only mean one thing. He didn't really believe Jeremy's death was a suicide either. June stopped mid-sentence and asked him how he knew about Felecia?

Will didn't come right out and say it but he did have some doubt about the circumstances surrounding Jeremy's death. He told June about the Rolling Stone magazine article. That it quoted her son saying life wasn't the same with his girlfriend gone.

"Your son told that magazine reporter that he missed his girlfriend, Mrs. London... He said she opened his eyes to the truth. That quote got me wondering what the essence of their relationship was, and if her leaving had anything to do with what happened to him. Would you happen to know where I might reach her?"

June hesitated. After the dream she'd had the night before she was quite sure she knew where Felecia was, and the detective wouldn't be reaching her anytime soon.

"She is dead, Detective," June answered. *"Felecia was killed by the same Satanic forces that murdered my son."* June went on to tell Will about the dream she'd had. She even named names, saying Elliot Prince, the CEO of her son's record company, had murdered Felecia in a sadistic ritual attended by dozens of fellow satanist.

"That is a very serious accusation, Mrs. London," Spider responded. *"You got any proof?"*

"The angel of the lord showed me, Detective," she replied. *"In a dream. That is all the proof I need. My son did not die in vain. His death will be vindicated on Judgement Day. My Jeremy was a hero. He refused the devil's enticement and paid the ultimate price, but his sacrifice will be honored in heaven."*

Will started to question his decision to call June London that morning. It sounded like she was a bit off her rocker. He did have some doubt about Jeremy London's death being a suicide but satanic human sacrifices and visits from angels? C'mon...That was not going to fly when it came time to request the case be reopened.

Will thanked June for the information, and told her he would be in touch. Just as he was about to hang up she dropped a bomb. *"Elliot Prince is here, Detective. He's here in New Smyrna Beach. My heathen husband went golfing with the bastard yesterday. I hope the hell he didn't invite him and his two cohorts to Jeremy's funeral next Thursday. That would be a huge mistake!"*

Spider asked June if he might be allowed to attend the service, and perhaps bring Carmella Henson? He wrote down the address of the church where the service was being held then hung up the phone. As he sat frozen to his sofa images of June's vision raced through his mind. Will imagined this Felecia Emmons lady must really be attractive to have enraptured the heart of an American Idol.

His calls to the LAPD missing persons unit came up empty. Spider contacted the Los Angeles Sound Engineers Union to try and find out if anyone there had seen or heard from Felecia, but no one had. He even talked to someone from the American Idol's television network hoping they might be able to help but no one had heard from her there either. Will even telephoned Head-Hunter Media Group thinking Felecia may be on their payroll. NADA...

People go missing all the time. Will knew that. If someone were so inclined it was possible to disappear without a trace and never be heard from again. But why would they? Why would she? Felecia appeared to have it made. Walking away from her life didn't make any sense. No more sense than Jeremy London killing himself... It was frightening to think June London could be right. But you had to wonder...

AN AMERICAN IDOL
The Illuminati Conspiracy

CHAPTER SEVENTEEN

The Illuminati. If someone were to find themselves in their grasp they would be hard pressed to escape. Truth is there would be no escaping. You don't just walk away from these people. If you lie down with the devil there is a very good chance you will get fucked. Sometimes those you love get fucked too.

All satanic groups have an agenda. To them people are just a means to an end, and the end always justifies the means. That is exactly how Felecia Emmons came to be victimized.

It happened slowly. Using recording engineer's lingo you could say that it happened *'adagio'* style. The tempo was barely noticeable. The moment Jeremy invited Felecia Emmons into his life the poor woman's days were numbered.

Felecia had managed to get herself hooked up with the American Idol family while she was still a junior in college. She wasn't the type you normally expect to see coming out of UCLA's School of Music. She was so down to earth and grounded. Perhaps it was her whole connection to the holistic way of life that made her seem so different and unique.

The woman did have an ear for music. She had an ear for the novel and the fresh. Felecia Emmons had the ability to pick up on the slightest nuance in a voice or an instrument where others failed to notice. She'd learned to zero in on those nuances, so much so her work became her life.

Sound reproduction connected Felecia Emmons to the universe. Her spirit itself could have been an onomastic synonym of a sound wave. In it she became one with nature. So when the opportunity to work the sound boards for 'American Idol' came up Felecia jumped at the chance. She had no way of knowing her decision would alter her life so drastically, though she did know it was possible...all things being connected.

For one thing her zip code changed. Before moving in with Jeremy Felecia had a small one bedroom flat in Montecito Heights, a middle class neighborhood north of downtown L.A. The place was clean and comfortable but lets face it, it wasn't Malibu.

When she moved in with Jeremy London Felecia's mornings started off with a brisk walk along the multicolored volcanic sands of Zuma Beach instead of a walk on her bedroom treadmill. Breakfast consisted of exotic fresh fruits and eggs benedict rather than a Denny's Grand Slam. When she ventured out it was behind the wheel of a brand new Land Rover, a gift from Jeremy to replace her five year old Honda Civic.

Still it was the music that mattered most. The luxuries were nice but they were just luxuries. Felecia wasn't brought up to be a material girl. She would have been just as content living in an RV and driving around on a scooter, as long as she had Jeremy and her work.

As for Jeremy, his music came from his gut. When he was first starting out in the business he insisted on not using software to produce idiosyncratic effects. He didn't like gimmicks. They could experiment with his sound if they wanted to, but rule number one was keep it real. Something changed that. Something Felecia didn't know about until it was too late.

One day Felecia received an unexpected visit from Elliot Prince. He showed up at her front door insisting they talk. Jeremy wasn't home at the time. He'd been scheduled to appear on a local television talk show to support an effort by a concerned citizens group to end racial profiling by police departments throughout L.A. County.

He'd gotten involved with the group after one of his session players was stopped and interrogated by police shortly after leaving a party at Jeremy's oceanfront home. The musician, who was black, was driving his Jaguar up the Pacific Coast Parkway when he saw the telltale flashing lights of the Highway Patrol. The officer who pulled him over ordered him to step out of his vehicle and put his hands on the hood of the patrol car. After roughly patting him down the officer placed him in handcuffs and put him in the backseat of the car.

When Jeremy found out that his guest had been manhandled by the police minutes after leaving his party he was appalled. Felecia told him about this guy she knew who belonged to a group fighting to end this type of behavior. She got in touch with him and the connection was made.

Elliot only learned about Jeremy's television interview after hearing about it from a colleague. He wasn't happy about not being brought into the loop. Contractually he had a right to approve or disapprove all Jeremy London appearances. Elliot was already suspicious that his singer wasn't living up to his end of the bargain from a musical standpoint.

He suspected Felecia had something to do with that. He needed her to stop infusing her unorthodox influences on Jeremy. The way he worded it, she was causing him a problem and that problem needed to go away. Elliot told Felecia he had big plans for Jeremy. He was going to use him to promote a world wide coming together of sorts. The Prince was adamant nothing was going to disrupt that plan.

He told Felecia her boyfriend had signed a new contract while she was up in San Francisco a few months back. He did not mention the two women he'd brought with him, or that they spent the night in her bed with Jeremy. He would hold onto that trump card just in case. He told Felecia Jeremy was legally bound to fulfill his obligations, and that not doing so would cause him irreparable harm.

"Our boy wonder is going to sing what he is told to sing," Elliot insisted. *"Head-Hunter Media produces his records. We have our own sound engineers. We don't need you interfering with our property. Is that understood, Ms. Emmons? Jeremy London is a business enterprise...and I own the franchise rights. Listen up little lady. You are treading on dangerous ground."*

Felecia had been in the business long enough to know how it works. She'd seen stars rise and watched them fall. She'd heard the rumors and suspected they were true. Except for the few who fall through the cracks every now and then Felecia knew it was those in control who determine who makes it and for how long.

Rumor was the entire music industry was controlled by a handful of very selfish men. Men with an extremely questionable agenda. The rumors always mentioned an agenda. No one ever mentioned the nature of that agenda. Now she knew...

Jeremy London was the undisputed King of Rock & Roll. His records consistently sat at the top of the charts. He wasn't just number one in America either. Jeremy was the most popular rock singer in the world. Six straight number ones, three straight multi-platinum selling albums, sold out stadiums everywhere he went. And the accolades didn't stop there. Jeremy had won several Grammy Awards, hosted SNL twice, and made guest appearances on all the network variety shows. He'd headlined the Super Bowl halftime show, and amassed a personal fortune of over forty-million dollars. And that figure was growing exponentially with every passing day.

But the entire thing could end as quickly as it started, and Felecia Emmons held the key. Jeremy would do whatever she told him to do. And The Prince knew it. That's what made her so dangerous. That's why he made several more trips to the Jeremy London home over the next few weeks. He wooed Felecia with promises of financial independence and professional advancement. He told her he would set her up in her own studio and provide her with a stable of artists on the cusp of stardom. She wouldn't need Jeremy. Felecia Emmons would be a bonafide player in the game. She would have complete artistic control over those in her stable. And all she had to do was persuade Jeremy not to bite the hand that feeds him.

The Prince could be very convincing. It took some doing but Felecia eventually agreed. It was with much trepidation she rendered up her soul to the demon that is Elliot Prince. She convinced herself she was doing it for Jeremy. She did not want him falling from grace just because she was a semanticist. You could say reality set in. Everyone has their price. When it comes down to it are we all not for sale to the highest bidder.

Felecia subtly encouraged Jeremy to let the professionals do what they do best. After all who were they to question Elliot Prince on technique and compositional content. The man was considered a genius in the music industry. If he wanted Jeremy to change his style why should they not consider it? She suggested his staying static was equivalent to falling behind.

So Jeremy allowed himself to be manipulated. He gave up artistic license over his music. He let Elliot Prince's technicians play around with his sound, and he sang the lyrics they gave him to sing. Any argument he could make would have been negated by the success of his next record. Sales went through the roof. The Elliot Prince collaboration went number one worldwide. *'Celluloid'* became the best selling rock album in history, easily passing AC/ DC's 'Back in Black.' The message was getting out. Their message. The Illuminati message. Subliminal as it was.

In the end Felecia remained true to her roots. If it hadn't been for the guilt she felt for deceiving the man she loved it would have been the disloyalty she felt towards herself. Fame and fortune almost always comes with conditions. Success undeserved does not provide true satisfaction, even if it results in personal gain. One still has to look in the mirror.

She stopped encouraging Jeremy to just go along. She knew he was unhappy, and she knew he was better than that. They discussed hiring a lawyer to see if there might be a loophole in Jeremy's recording contract. One that would allow him to regain some control over his music. They secretly laid down tracks for a new album, with all words and music written by Jeremy. The tapes would need to be digitally mixed with other instruments but it was a step in the right direction.

Unfortunately Elliot Prince proved impatient. With the enormous success of 'Celluloid' under his belt he thought his plan ingenious. It had become obvious that Felecia Emmons was no longer playing the game. The foolish tart was a radical extremist in a pacifist body. The time for action had come

AN AMERICAN IDOL
The Illuminate Conspiracy

CHAPTER EIGHTEEN

Thursday morning was an unusually warm day for the dead of winter in central Florida. Temperatures were in the upper eighties. This was a day that June London had always feared. Her unsaved son had beaten her to the grave. June's hope was that the Lord would honor Jeremy's refusal to bow to the forces of evil and welcome him into the kingdom anyway.

It was fortunate the family had been able to keep the funeral plans secret, despite the daily throng of reporters who'd shown up at their door. June's pastor had even managed to keep details of the service from the rest of his congregation, many of whom would have been excited by the prospect of attending the singer's funeral.

The only guests the family invited was a handful of relatives who'd flown in for the occasion and a few close family friends. If Detective Durance and Ms. Henson showed up they'd be welcome of course, but that was it.

Knowing her husband, June wondered if the fool might have spilled the beans about the location of the funeral to Elliot Prince and his friends. After the dream she had she was praying the man wouldn't show up. She couldn't be responsible for how she might react.

Of course Prince had every intention of being there. This funeral was to be an Illuminati affair. And though it would remain a small private service there was certain protocol that must be adhered to. It had been the same deal at other Illuminati celebrations. The Lady Bird funeral, the Mandela bash, Whitney's Hall of Fame party. Symbolism was and always will be an important part of The Illuminati's agenda, albeit it much of it subliminally disseminated. The average person wouldn't notice, but those in the know definitely would.

Pentecostal Assembly Church sits just across from the new public library in New Smyrna Beach. Thanks to a ten foot tall hedgerow of Seagrape it is well hidden from the heavy traffic that tends to fly down Old Dixie Highway most days. Those not familiar with the area have to keep a close watch for the church's street sign. If they wait until they see it it's too late. They will have to continue down the highway and make a U-turn.

June and her husband arrived at the church right on time. They sat in the pastor's office drinking iced tea while he reviewed the agenda he had outlined for the service with them. It was pretty basic. There would be a few moments of personal introspection followed by a reading from the book of Psalms. Then the church's musical director would play a selection he picked out on his guitar.

At that point the pastor will approach the podium and give his eulogy. He will follow that up with a passage from the New Testament. Then a prayer will be offered, followed by an opportunity for anyone in attendance to stand and say a few words of endearment. At the end of the service people will be welcome to come forward to pay their last respects to the deceased.

Because of the limited number of people invited to attend the service a small reception would be held in the cafe immediately following the service. The actual burial would be held later in the day at an undisclosed location with only the immediate family in attendance.

Considering who was being buried, and the enormous wealth he'd accumulated, the funeral plans seemed quite paltry. Jeremy London was loved by millions of people all over the world. News of his death had shaken his fans, who simply couldn't understand why their idol would take his own life. They'd want him to have a grand send off. Some thought his body should have been laid in state so his fans could line up to pay homage.

That's what Jeremy's father would have done. Larry London didn't agree with his wife about the privacy thing. His son was an international superstar. He deserved to be recognized for his accomplishments. Who cared if the paparazzi showed up to film the event? Why not have droves of fans winding their way out of the parking lot and down Old Dixie Highway waiting for a chance to show their last respects? There could have been a long drawn out processional. A parade of famous dignitaries all there to honor his son.

He never questioned it verbally. June was in charge. He knew that. She always had been. In the London home she ruled the roost.

They'd met at college. Florida Southern University. While attending a basketball game no less. They had both just witnessed their team beat Nova University in double overtime. The victory assured the small private school the conference championship and a spot in the NCAA Division II tournament.

The entire student section was in delirium. Everybody in attendance hugged everybody else who was there. Larry happened to be sitting directly behind June at the time. He leaned forward and planted a big kiss right on her lips. It was typical Larry London behavior, but for June it was anything but. She had dated a few boys, all of whom her mother approved of in advance, but June was not yet sexually active. She found Larry's forwardness to be quite extreme, and unexpectedly exciting.

So she kissed him back. While everyone else was jumping up and down celebrating the small school's victory June lost herself in Larry's arms. Three months later they were married.

FSU ended up winning the NCAA Division II championship that year. As a matter of fact the school won a sports triple crown of sorts. They also won the 1981 Division II championship in men's golf and baseball. No school has repeated that feat since.

After college Larry and June settled in the Jacksonville, Florida area. He went to work for Fidelity Trust Bank while June went on to earn her masters degree in elementary education. They purposefully put off starting a family. June would have loved to have a child but Larry had other plans.

From day one of their marriage both June and Larry concentrated on their own personal interests. Larry joined a men's bowling league and played softball in his downtime, while June took to gardening. She turned their quarter acre suburban lot into a virtual haven for butterflies. She planted Sea Holly, Zinnia, Snapdragons, Coneflower, and anything else that would help attract the colorful winged fairies. And oh yes, she also got saved.

Like most Americans June grew up in a Christian home. Her family attended the United Methodist Church. That meant she learned about sanctification and the gifts of the Spirit early on. When a teacher friend of hers invited her to attend a Pentecostal Revival Meeting taking place in a neighboring town June actually got to see some of those gifts displayed.

Back in the mid 1980s a Holy Ghost revival of sorts sprang up in the city of Palatka, Florida. Word is a traveling preacher happened to be passing through town one day when he was flagged down by a distressed woman standing on the side of the road. The woman had been rushing her fifteen year old pregnant daughter to the hospital because the girl had gone into labor when her daughter suddenly screamed, *"Mommy, the baby is coming out."*

The woman stopped the car right there in the middle of the road and jumped out. Moments later the traveling preacher happened by. Seeing the woman standing in the middle of the road he pulled over, not knowing what to expect. He found the pregnant teenager in the back seat of her mother's car with a newborn infant at her feet. The child appeared to be stillborn. It wasn't breathing and it had turned blue. The preacher climbed into the back seat of the car and laid hands on the dead infant.

According to witnesses this went on for close to ten minutes. The esoteric preacher just refused to give up. He prayed intercession over the lifeless newborn, calling on the Lord for mercy and claiming the child for Christ. Just as an ambulance arrived the child started breathing. When paramedics rushed over to the car they stood there scratching their heads in bewilderment. They'd expected to find a dead newborn in the car. This child appeared perfectly normal.

It was this same preacher who started the Pentecostal Assembly Church in Palatka, Florida. When word of the miracle on State Route 100 got out it spread like wildfire. The preacher was assured a large crowd would attend if he were to get permission from the city to hold a revival. Three days after laying hands on that newborn baby a huge tent went up on River Street just beyond the railroad tracks. Over one thousand people showed up, all seeking miracles of their own. The rest is history.

It was three months after that miraculous event that June and her friend visited Palatka. The charismatic tent preacher was preaching to thousands by then. People from all over the United States came to witness miracles and be healed. It was from this humble beginning that the Pentecostal Assembly Church in New Smyrna Beach sprung from. The church June currently attends.

June saw people speaking in tongues that night. She witnessed people being slain in the spirit and cripples in wheelchairs going forward to receive healing. A few of them walked out of that tent on their own two feet. When June left the meeting later that night she was a changed person. Something had been revealed to her. From that moment on June London dedicated her life to serving God.

His wife's devout Christianity drove Larry London nuts. She was already something of a prude when he met her. After she got saved June became even more puritanical and condescending. She was constantly pointing out her husband's faults. Telling him he was living in sin and needed to repent. Her patronizing behavior nearly drove him away. Then she got pregnant.

The marriage went from bad to worse. The two of them headed off in totally opposite directions. June became even more introspective. She spent most of her free time studying the word and praying. Her position as a school teacher became a point of contention too. When she wasn't studying her concordance she was formulating her classroom syllabus.

As for Larry, he spent more and more time on his hobbies. He took up target shooting as a way of releasing stress, and he bought golf clubs. Guns and golf became his obsession. When he wasn't firing his pistols at the range he was out on a golf course somewhere. When he was home he was watching golf on television. Neither he nor June took to parenting. Shortly after Jeremy was born a nanny was hired.

It was four years later the London family moved to New Smyrna Beach. Larry's former employer up in Jacksonville consolidated with another bank and downsized operations. He found a new job with an investment brokerage firm in New Smyrna. June wasn't happy about being forced to give up her teaching position so they could move. The only saving grace was the fact Pentecostal Assembly was expanding and planned to build a new church there.

Somehow the family survived. Three people living under one roof, sharing meals and ignoring each other. For the most part Jeremy spent his early childhood unaware that his family was dysfunctional. It wasn't until he was older that it became apparent. That's when he bought his first guitar.

When Detective Durance arrived for the funeral service he found a shady parking spot in the corner of the lot. He'd invited Carmella to join him. She was dressed in a silk knee length black dress and matching high heels. A large leather handbag hung from her right shoulder, bouncing against her hip with every step she took across the parking lot. Spider's eyes were drawn to the distraction, though he tried to conceal his interest.

They were half way across the lot when Will decided it was too darn hot for a suit coat. He told Carmella to go on ahead and he'd catch up. Then he peeled off his jacket and hustled back to the car. The detective was wearing a shoulder holster underneath his jacket. Spider preferred to use the shoulder holster to conceal his weapon rather than keep it behind his back or beneath his trousers. Realizing he probably shouldn't attend a funeral with his gun exposed he removed the holster and tossed it into the glove box. He wouldn't be needing it today.

As Will made his way back toward the entrance of the church a limousine pulled into the parking lot. The chauffeur drove his limo right up to the front door. Spider assumed the car belonged to the funeral home so he was surprised when four impeccably dressed men climbed out.

One of them appeared to be in charge. The guy was dressed in an obviously expensive black pinstripe suit. The detective knew it was a Hugo Boss by the emblem on the man's belt buckle. He was also wearing a white gold Rolex around this wrist, suggesting he was quite well off.

To further flaunt his affluence the guy wore a gaudy ring on the middle finger of his left hand. It featured a beautifully sculpted green lion made from pure jade. He also wore a fancy pin on his lapel. It depicted a blue eyed white snow owl. The owl's eyes appeared to be cut from blue diamonds. An even closer inspection would have revealed the diamonds were cut into shapes. The letters B and C.

The average Joe wouldn't recognize the symbolism. It would take one to know one. The jade lion represented alchemy. One of the steps that lead to illumination. The snow owl represented wisdom. Something the early Catholic Church did not want its followers to possess. The letters on the snow owl's blue diamond eyes stood for Bavarian Club, the original Freemason organization from which the Illuminati had its origins.

The guy in charge motioned for his entourage to follow him inside. Will followed close behind. A mahogany table had been set up in the vestibule just outside the sanctuary. A registry book sat on top, along with a pen attached by a long cord. Spider waited patiently while the men from the limo signed the book.

He thought he recognized one of them. This one guy looked a lot like Richard Tejada, Florida's lieutenant-governor. He was rather on the chubby side like Tejada was, and of Latino descent. Thing is this guy was coddling the man who was in charge as if he was the guy's manservant. Spider knew the Richard Tejada he knew would never behave in such a manner. No way. In fact he would be the one being coddled.

Once the gang of four had signed in it was Will's turn. As he stood looking down at the registry the detective noted there were thirteen names scribbled on the page. Carmella Henson was number seven. Spider signed the book then scanned the page to see if it could have possibly been the lieutenant-governor he'd followed into the church.

To his surprise it was. The politician had signed his given name, Juan De'Ricardo Tejada, but it was definitely him. Spider wondered who the hell it was the lieutenant-governor was accompanying. Whoever it was the guy must be Goddamned important if he had someone like Richard Tejada kowtowing to him.

Will reviewed the other names on the list. The guy in charge had signed in first. It looked like his name was Stanley...or maybe it was Stanton, it was hard to read the signature. The last name was definitely Price. In either case it wasn't anyone he'd ever heard of before. Spider checked the other signatures.

Cecille D'ville had signed his name in concise clear script. The only signature that stayed within the lines. The man had also added the designation Esq. after his name. So he was an attorney.

The last signature was E. Prince. Spider assumed the E stood for Elliot. Elliot Prince, the famous Hollywood record producer. Will had certainly heard of him. The guy was supposedly the most successful record producer in American history.

Will found Carmella sitting at the rear of the sanctuary. The London family was gathered together in the first row. Invited friends and colleagues sat behind them. The gang of four Will had followed inside were seated on the opposite side of the church but towards the front. Those already seated took no notice of them.

Jeremy Tobias London lay in a coffin at the front of the sanctuary. The casket lid was open but no one went forward to view the body at this point. Classical music played in the background as the last of the late arrivals took their seats. At the conclusion of the cantata a woman approached the podium. She thanked everyone for coming then said the family had requested we take a few moments to remember Jeremy London in our prayers. With that she turned and walked off the stage.

You could hear the silence of the hushed crowd. A few restrained coughs. People shuffling in their seats. Murmured whispers. After a moment the woman reappeared. She opened her bible and read a passage from the old testament. Will found it interesting that she had chosen the 56th Psalm.

"They gather themselves together. They hide themselves and mark my steps. They wait for my soul..."

When the woman finished reading the passage a guitarist walked out from behind the curtain and stood along the side of the stage. The church's musical director introduced himself then proceeded to sing a song. He said it was an ode to a musician gone home.

*"I want to wear a crown of glory...
When I get home to that good land...
I want to shout salvation's story...
In concert with that blood-washed band."*

At the conclusion of the song another man appeared, this time from the back of the stage. He approached the podium and introduced himself. Pastor Carter wore a broad grin on his face. His eyes sparkled and he conveyed confidence. He was short statured, with thinning dark hair. He scanned the assembled crowd, purposely making eye contact with as many as would allow. Then he spoke.

"Good afternoon, Dear friends. May God bless you on this glorious day. We have gathered together to celebrate the life of our brother Jeremy Tobias London, who has gone to be with the Lord Jesus Christ. Today Jeremy is in heaven, free of the trials and travails of this life. And though we will miss him we know Jeremy lives on in glory".

The pastor stopped to take a swig of water from a glass sitting on top of the podium then continued. *"Picture yourselves standing along the shore looking out at the horizon. You see a ship in the distance and watch as it sails out of sight. As you bid that ship farewell there are those on the opposite shore that wait to welcome it when it comes into view. Those aboard that ship have left us for a while but they will be received on the other side with open arms. And so it is with our Jeremy. You see we live in an imperfect world ladies and gentlemen. In a world populated by imperfect people. Today Jeremy Tobias London has become perfection. So as we come together know not to mourn his passing but to celebrate his victory... Amen."*

At the conclusion of the service those in attendance were informed that the actual burial was to be a private affair. They were invited to come forward and pay their last respects to the deceased before the body was removed in preparation for burial. About a half dozen people did. June London remained seated as they filed past her. She knew them all, but one. A tall man in a very expensive pinstripe suit.

When the man approached Jeremy's casket he lingered awhile. He didn't speak. He just stood there looking down at Jeremy as if waiting for him to open his eyes and sit up. Finally the man bent over and kissed Jeremy's ice cold cheek.

None of the locals knew Stanton Price, Jr. Nor did any of them know why he was there. They didn't know he was a man of his word, and that to him a promise made is a promise kept. With one undetected motion Stanton had snuck the vial containing a portion of Felecia Emmons cremated remains inside Jeremy's coffin. The portion being her reproductive organs if his wishes had been carried out. Considering the sacrifice she'd made for the cause it was the least he could do. The deed done, he turned to leave.

As he did June London locked eyes with the stranger and the picture became clear. She knew what was happening. She began to shake as fear replaced the shock that shot through her body when she realized the man standing in front of her son's casket was the man from her dreams. The one who'd overseen Felecia Emmon's vicious rape and murder. The man who'd appeared on the screens in that awful place where people were forced into the abyss. But then June's fear morphed into anger. Her trembling hands stopped shaking and dropped from her face to her lap. Then to the purse she held on her lap. What happened next might very well have been avoided if someone had only listened to her sooner.

AN AMERICAN IDOL
The Illuminati Conspiracy
CHAPTER NINETEEN

It was Carmella Henson who acted first. She watched in disbelief as June London pulled a gun from her purse and pointed it at the well dressed man standing in front of her son's casket. The former police officer turned victim's advocate reacted as she'd been trained. She always carried a weapon, even when off duty. Without having to think about it first she pulled the snub nosed revolver out of her handbag and shouted a warning.

But the distraught mother wouldn't be denied. June London didn't know who exactly this man was, but she knew he was evil. She knew in her heart this man with the fancy jewelry was the person responsible for her son's death. She knew Jeremy did not hang himself. This motherfucker murdered him.

As mourners ran from the sanctuary June remained frozen in place, as did Stanton Price, Jr. Will cursed himself for leaving his weapon in his car. He never should have taken off his jacket. Damn the Florida heat. He watched helplessly as Carmella took control of the situation.

"Drop your weapon, Mrs. London. DO IT NOW," she demanded. *"If you force me to I will blow your Goddamn head off... Do you understand me, June... Now Drop It!"*

Off to the side Elliot Prince stood with his cohorts watching the event transpire. He felt as helpless as Detective Durance did, but unlike the detective he WAS packing. Elliot always carried a weapon on him. In his line of work it was a necessity. There were a lot of crazy bastards in L.A. Especially in the music industry. He didn't want to make matters worse but there was no way he was going to let this woman shoot the Grand Pindar of The Illuminati.

Before leaving home June had rummaged through her husband's gun collection and picked out a piece she thought would do the job, had the job become necessary. She'd never fired a weapon in her life but she was quite certain she could hit a target at this close range. Until that moment she'd assumed the target would be Elliot Prince. If the bastard even dared to show up at her son's funeral that is. The very last thing she expected was to be face to face with the man from her dreams. She didn't even know his name.

Larry couldn't believe this was happening. June wasn't a killer. She might pray you to death, but she wouldn't shoot you. How the hell did she get her hands on his gun anyway? The 357 magnum she brought to that church today would blow a man's face off. He was surprised the fucking thing would fit in her purse. It had a five inch barrel and weighed nearly two pounds. Larry knew the revolver could fire eight shots. He slowly started to creep his way down the pew and away from the line of fire.

What happened next happened almost simultaneously. It started with a smile. A frigid foreboding smile that could have been a precursor of what was to come. The grin on Stanton's face was the match that lit the fuse. If June London had any doubt about what she was doing that fucking grin wiped it away. You'd have thought a man staring down the barrel of a Smith and Wesson 38 caliber revolver pointed at the precise spot where his eyebrows join together might show some fear. Not Stanton Price, Jr. He just grinned.

June's hands began to tremble as she pulled back on the trigger.

Her husband's gun weighed heavy in her small hands. Beads of sweat began to roll down her forehead, burning her eyes and slightly blinding her.

Foreseeing the distraught woman was actually going to fire her weapon Elliot Prince reached inside his jacket and pulled out his. A stainless steel high performance Rugar SR40. The gun was known to be deadly accurate. Fortunately it didn't have to be be. Carmella Henson fired first.

The victim advocate's bullet tore through the back of June London's head and lodged in her brain at precisely the same moment June got off her round. The would be assassin dropped to the floor like a heavy sack of marbles. She was dead before her head ever hit the floor.

The shot June London managed to get off missed its mark. The recoil from her weapon was enough to alter the bullet's projection. Just enough. An experienced shooter would have expected the kickback action and prepared himself for it. Not June. Her choice of weapon probably saved her intended victim's life. Had she gone with a weapon of smaller caliber the grieving mother may very well have been successful.

Detective Durance ran over and picked up the gun June had fired, then checked her wrist for a pulse. There was none. The detective looked over at Stanton Price, who by then had rejoined his colleagues on the opposite side of the church. *"Why would she want to kill you, Sir,"* Will asked him? *"Who the hell are you?"*

Stanton told Will he had no idea why the woman would want to kill him. He said he didn't even know the woman. He'd simply chosen to attend the funeral out of respect for his friend Elliot Prince, Jeremy London's record producer. He admitted knowing who the woman's husband was, having teamed up with him on a golf outing earlier in the week.

"Larry and I only just met that day," Stanton explained. *"I told him I was a fan of his son's music and offered to help with the funeral expenses. It had not yet occurred to me the man would probably be inheriting his son's fortune. He'd have no need for my help anytime soon. It was a gesture of good will. Not very well received, or so it seems."*

Just then a police SWAT team burst into the room. It took a few minutes before word was passed that the emergency was over. After sorting out what had happened they all left, replaced by a team of homicide detectives and various personnel from forensics.

Carmella Henson was visibly shaken by the turn of events. After eleven years in uniform and another fourteen as a victim advocate she'd never had to discharge her weapon. Shooting a woman in the back of the head at her own child's funeral was not something you'd ever expect or prepare for. Had there been any way to avoid it she certainly would have.

A follow up investigation conducted by internal affairs and the State of Florida exonerated Carmella of any wrongdoing. She'd acted professionally and appropriately to a deadly situation and was to be commended. It was determined her actions in all probability saved the lives of countless innocent victims, most notably Stanton Price, Jr.

She and Detective William Durance had attended the funeral after being invited by the deceased man's family. They were there as guests. Neither of them was serving in any official capacity, nor was there any ongoing investigations being conducted by the Daytona Beach Police Department. The Volusia County Medical Examiner's Office had determined Jeremy London's death was a suicide. Barring any new evidence to the contrary the case was closed.

AN AMERICAN IDOL
The Illuminati Conspiracy)

CHAPTER TWENTY

Life goes on. Two years after the incident at the funeral home Will Durance became Detective Sergeant of the police department's homicide division. A year later he teamed up with renowned psychic and national television personality Jordan Downs to solve a serial murder case involving teenage boys. A couple of retired guys from New Jersey had rented an oceanfront condo and were luring teenage boys to their apartment with offers of drugs and cash. They'd sit on their balcony and scan the beach for potential targets. Six boys disappeared before the two were finally caught.

As it turned out the sick bastards were sexually molesting the boys then taking them out on a boat where they would chop them up into little pieces and feed them to the sharks.

Carmella Henson retired from her job as a victim advocate. She'd given twenty-five years of her life to the department. That was enough. She went to bartender school and earned a certificate as a professional mixologist. She likes to tell her friends that going to bartender school was a colossal waste of time because despite all the knowledge she acquired there is still only one drink she makes perfectly. A dirty martini...

Carmella eventually did have Detective Durance over for one of her special dirty martinis. He even got to admire the Toulouse Lautrec hanging on Carmella's bedroom wall. He found *'Femmes de Maison'* to be truly inspiring...

Larry London inherited the bulk of his son's estate. Jeremy had amassed a fortune totaling over forty million dollars in his short illustrious career. Larry spent ten million of it on a twelve thousand square foot beachfront mansion, then filled his expansive garage with sports cars. He purchased a Ferrari, a Porsche Carrera, a Bugatti SS, and his favorite, a classic 1966 Corvette Stingray. Larry also bought himself a brand new Harley. A customized fifty-thousand dollar Ultra Limited. And oh yes, he also got remarried.

Larry London's new wife was nothing like his first. June had driven Larry crazy with all her praying and rejoicing and speaking in tongues. This one was no bother at all. She couldn't be. She was hardly ever home. Taylor Louise was something of a *'freebird'*. A world traveler and dedicated shopaholic. She loved to grace the shops of Paris, London, and Rome with her presence. Every couple of weeks she'd come home for a spell. Mostly to unpack her bags. Then she'd be off again.

Larry continued golfing. In fact he purchased a thirty-six hole golf course up in Palm Coast. That piece of real estate set him back a cool eighteen million dollars. But he got to go golfing whenever he wanted. Life was good...

Until the day came it dawned on Larry that maybe he was spending his inheritance a little too quickly and if he didn't get it under control it would be gone in no time. Of course the answer to his problem wasn't for him to cut back his spending. it was for his new wife to. That didn't go over to well. Once Taylor Louise's wings were clipped and she was put on a limited budget she become disenchanted and filed for a divorce.

She wanted the beach house, Ferrari, and an allowance sufficient enough o keep her in the lifestyle she'd grown accustomed to.They settled out of court, with Taylor Louise getting exactly what she asked for. The house, the Ferrari, and a four million dollar cash buyout. Larry did get to keep his prized Chevy Corvette and the golf course. Unfortunately he'd hired an old boss of his to manage the course. The guy was supposedly a financial wizard. Larry used to work for him at Fidelity Trust Bank when they lived in Jacksonville. The man had been a successful senior money manager there. Larry knew the guy was really good at showing people how to invest their money wisely in order to get the best return on their investment.

Hiring his former boss to manage his golf course turned out to be an even worse decision than his marrying Taylor Louise. The guy ended up embezzling seven million dollars from Larry before he was caught. If it hadn't been for an IRS audit the guy would probably still be transferring Larry's funds to an offshore bank account he'd set up to hide his illicit activities.

His inheritance all but gone now Larry turned to a friend for advice. Florida Lieutenant-Governor Richard Tejada. He and the lieutenant governor had kept in touch after what happened at his son's funeral. Both men shared a real passion for golf. Tejada had traveled over to Palm Coast to play Larry's course a number of times. Larry had even supported the man financially when Tejada ran for the United States Congress. Despite Larry's sizable donation Tejada lost that election. But it was very close. Just a twelve-hundred vote margin.

Such a close loss would have been debilitating for many politicians but not for Richard Tejada. The portly politician used the experience as inspiration to try for even loftier goals. The presidential primaries were coming up at the end of January and a number of people in very high places were offering to support his campaign were he to run. Stanton Price, Jr. being among them. After hearing how Larry had been screwed over by his business associate to the point of being destitute the lieutenant-governor put his friend to work on his campaign.

Larry must have been blinded by ignorance. Either that or he was just plain out of touch with reality, because losing the entire fortune he'd inherited from his son hardly seemed to faze him. Truth is Larry didn't really miss the money. He missed June... He missed knowing someone was there. Someone reliable. Someone he could point to with pride and say, "She's with me." If only he'd done that when she was alive.

Larry was in Naples working on the Tejada for President campaign when he received word his son had just been elected to the Rock and Roll Hall of Fame. The news came as a total surprise because according to the rules Hall of Fame nominees aren't even eligible for consideration until twenty-five years after the release of their first recording. Jeremy had been dead for less than six years and it had only been eight since the release of his first record, 'Hell on Wheels.'

He would of course receive the award posthumously. Elliot Prince was working behind the scenes to make sure everything fell into place. He was putting together a greatest hits album to coincide with the event, as well as a Jeremy London 'Live' concert tour. The plan was to create a digitally enhanced hologram of Jeremy, only this one would be bigger, better, and more controllable than the original. If it all went as planned the projects could earn him tens of millions of dollars, and depending on the response much more than that. The sky was literally the limit.

A full length movie of Jeremy's life was also in the works. It was to be a big budget affair with top stars playing the lead roles. The Prince was planning to market all sorts of products to coincide with the film's release. People would be able to purchase Jeremy London eye wear, Jeremy London cologne. Even Jeremy London guitars. A line of Jeremy London clothing was also being developed. Hats and jackets and T-shirts. Things like that. Elliot Prince was planning to promote the whole Jeremy Tobias London affair as the second coming.

The Rock and Roll Hall of Fame had been lobbied hard to make an exception to its rules concerning induction. The process had always been shrouded in controversy anyway. Questionable selections had been made while obvious choices were left out. In Jeremy's case they got smart. They used the Hall of Fame's own rules against them. Specifically the one that demanded musical excellence be the main criteria for selection. It was hard to make an argument against allowing the exception and after some debate the judges made their decision.

The Rock and Roll Hall of Fame is located in Cleveland, Ohio but the ceremony honoring the inductees takes place in Los Angeles. The event is aired on national television. This year advertising spots were being sold for as much or more than sponsors paid for Super Bowl commercials. It was insane... The entire country was going crazy for Jeremy London all over again.

How did this happen? Who changed the rules? Questions were coming from the four corners of the country. Traditionalist wanted to know who was responsible. Why have rules if they are subject to change by whoever complains the loudest? Of course the answer was quite simple. THEY DID!

There it was again. Who killed Jeremy London? THEY DID! Who killed John F. Kennedy? THEY DID! How about John Lennon, Whitney Houston. Kurt Cobain.

Larry London was invited to attend the festivities. As a matter of fact Elliot Prince wanted Jeremy's father on the stage with him when the award was presented. Richard Tejada should be there too. The publicity would be great for his presidential run. The ceremony was scheduled to be aired the night of January 23rd. One week before the California presidential primary on January 31st. With luck and hard work they would all be partying like it was 1999 all over again.

AN AMERICAN IDOL
The Illuminati Conspiracy

CHAPTER TWENTY-ONE

Samsula Self Storage is located on State Route 415 about half a mile north of the Volusia County Landfill. Larry drove out to the facility to retrieve some personal items he'd stored there just before marrying his second wife. Taylor Louise would never have allowed them in the house. Not that she said so. Larry just knew.

Taylor Louise wasn't the type of person to acknowledge her new husband may have had a life before hooking up with her. It was okay to mention his son Jeremy, but he knew better than to bring up his first wife. Having photos of June in the house would have been disastrous. Larry was certain they would have been destroyed.

It had been a few years since he'd been out to that storage facility. Larry always made sure the space was paid for every month but he never had any reason to visit it. The sixty square foot metal locker was hallowed ground. If Jeremy's fans ever discovered its existence they'd be sure to vandalize it. That's why Larry chose this particular facility. There wasn't anything else around for miles, meaning no foot traffic or snooping eyes.

His son's boyhood was in those boxes. Jeremy's elementary school report cards and bowling trophies. His first baby shoes and baseball mitt. They were all out there. As were Larry's old wedding pictures and Father's Day cards, not to mention his collection of pistols.

Larry hadn't handled one of his guns since the day his wife snuck one of them out of the house fully intending to use it to kill someone. That was nearly six years ago now. The day of Jeremy's funeral. A police psychologist suggested June may have suffered from PTSD. Post Traumatic Stress Disorder. Losing her only child had simply been more than she could handle. Especially considering it had been by suicide. A mother can feel a lot of guilt over that.

The revolver she used to try and shoot Stanton Price, Jr. was back in its box now, having been returned by the police department some six months after the event took place. And there it would remain.

After rummaging around in the storage locker awhile Larry finally found what he was looking for. A cardboard box with PHOTOS written across it in big block letters. He carried the heavy box out to his Corvette and set it down on the passenger seat then went back inside to lock up. When he came back a sheriff's deputy was there waiting for him. The deputy had his patrol car right up against Larry's front bumper. He looked at Larry and said, *"That's a fine looking ride you got there, Sir. She yours?"*

Larry chuckled. Was the Corvette his? That cherry red Corvette was the last remaining thing he owned on the face of the fucking earth. Taylor Louise had sucked him dry. And what she didn't take his business manager did. *"Yep, she sure is"* he answered. *"Bought and paid for with blood, sweat, and tears."* And truer words were never spoken.

The deputy stepped out of his patrol car and slowly walked over to the passenger side of Larry's Corvette, then peered inside. *"What's in the box,"* he asked?

Larry tried to explain why he was there. He told the deputy the box contained only personal items. Some old photographs, some college textbooks, his son's high school yearbook.

"You got I.D." the deputy asked?

Larry pulled out his wallet and handed it to the deputy as he said, *"Look Officer, my name is Larry London. You're a relatively young man. You may have heard of my son. He was a singer... Jeremy London? The rock musician? You watch American Idol?"*

Of course the deputy had heard of him. Everyone around here knew who Jeremy London was. And everyone knew about the shooting that took place at his son's funeral over in New Smyrna Beach.

"You telling me your wife is the one who tried to shoot that rich dude at the funeral that day? you saying it was her that got shot dead by that police woman advocate? Damn, what the fuck was wrong with her, man? Was them two of having an affair or something? You can level with me... Bro."

Larry just shook his head. His wife have an affair? If this dumb ass cop only knew. That woman wouldn't have an affair with Elvis Presley, much less some rich old fart from California. Her pussy belonged to Jesus Christ. Hell he didn't even get any of that pussy the last few years of their marriage.

The deputy went on to tell Larry there had been a few break ins out there lately. That's why he was patrolling the area. He joked about some thief looking for the Holy Grail. He said one brother had gotten away with somebody's expensive table lamps and a karaoke machine... *"Ain't nobody reported no Holy Grail missing though... Least not yet!"*

With that the deputy climbed in his patrol car and backed up. He pulled alongside Larry's corvette and rolled down his window again, then said, *"Tell me something, Mr. London. Is it true your son is being inducted into the Rock & Roll Hall of Fame? Maybe I should be asking you for your autograph!"*

"Maybe you should" Larry replied. *"That and a five dollar note might get you a one way ticket on the Sunrail train to Sanford."* The comment brought a smile to both men's lips.

Larry was staying at a motel on US 1 just south of the New Smyrna Beach line. The place was built back in the early 1950's before I-95 went in. Anyone driving to or from Miami would have had to pass right by it. It was called The Sea Garden Inn. The motel had sixteen units, each one came with a small fridge, microwave, and cable television. Not bad for forty-two bucks a night.

The minute Larry got back to his room he tore into the cardboard box he retrieved from the storage unit. Three photo albums lay at the bottom of the box, like anchors securing the life he once had. The life he came to realize much too late he never fully appreciated. Larry London was emotionally moored to those old photo albums. It was as if their very existence justified his.

On top of the photo albums was his son's high school yearbook. Larry bypassed that and reached instead for an old textbook he'd kept from college. Larry had taken a writing course his senior year at

Florida Southern. The class had been taught by a visiting professor named Jonathan Hayes. The very same Jonathan Hayes who won an Academy Award back in 1954 for writing the screenplay for the Alfred Hitchcock film, *'Rear Window.'*

Hayes had also collaborated on other Alfred Hitchcock films, most notably *'To Catch a Thief'* and *'The Man Who Knew Too Much.'* He was quite a brilliant man, and kind enough to sign one of Larry London's textbooks. It became one of Larry's prize possessions.

Larry recalled the day he'd brought all that stuff out to the storage unit. He didn't want to part with his old picture albums or the other memorabilia so renting a storage space made sense. While sitting there reminiscing he suddenly remembered he'd stuffed his wife's bible in that same box before sealing it. Lord knows he couldn't have kept that at the house. Taylor Louise would have thrown a fit. Larry felt his way around the sides of the box until he found the leather bound bible. It was laying on its side pressed up against the photo albums.

He opened it up and fingered through it. June had often used a yellow highlighter when studying to underline certain verses. She would often scribble little notes on the bottoms of certain pages too. Her writing was difficult to read. In some cases impossible. But it was there. Most of her notes dealt with the same theme. The battle between good and evil.

Larry climbed into bed with his wife's bible. After fluffing a couple of pillows behind his head he opened it up and started reading where June had highlighted in yellow. First the Gospels, then the epistles of Paul.

In the fourth chapter of Mathew he read, *"And the devil said to him I will give the kingdoms of the world to he who worships me."*

When Larry got to the thirteenth chapter of Mark he saw June had underlined the verse, *"False prophets will appear performing signs and wonders hoping to lead you astray."*

Then again in the gospel of John, *"Light shines on the darkness. The darkness cannot overcome it."*

As Larry read the highlighted scriptures something happened inside him. Something deep down in his soul. He could feel the Spirit of the Lord moving through him.

The words he was reading weren't the first time he had heard them. June had ranted that same dogma time and time again when she was alive. This time though the words seemed to speak life to him. He continued reading.

Jude, chapter 1; *"Certain people will creep in unnoticed. Ungodly people. People who will try to pervert God's plan."*

In Ephesians, chapter 5 June had underlined, *"Take no part in the works of darkness. Instead, expose them."*

Then again in Ephesians, chapter 6; *"Our battle is not against flesh and blood but against the powers of this present darkness. Our struggle is with the forces of evil."*

Larry climbed out of bed and dropped to his knees, then began weeping uncontrollably. Like so many others before him he was finally coming to terms with his sin. When that happens, when someone finally surrenders and admits they can't do it on their own, it is an extremely emotional moment. June had been trying to tell her husband that for years, if only he'd listened.

The truth is Larry thought she was delusional. All that mumbo jumbo about the wages of sin being death. How satanic forces were trying to bring destruction to mankind. He figured she was off her rocker. And now here he was, on his knees blathering away like a baby. Tears rolling down his cheeks as he begged the Lord for forgiveness. He confessed the error of his ways and asked God to reveal the truth. The truth his wife had seemed to know all along.

An hour later Larry was back in bed feverishly fingering through the rest of the new testament. He searched every page for the clues his wife had left him all those years ago. Highlighted in yellow marker to make his journey easier.

1st John, chapter 5 said, *"The world is under the power of the evil one."*

In 1st Peter, chapter 5 Larry read, *"Your adversary the devil prowls around like a roaring lion seeking to devour you."*

Again in 2nd Peter, chapter 2; *"They will try to entice you. They will promise you freedom, but they are corrupt. Whomever overcomes a person, to them that person is enslaved."*

It was a sleepless night. A million thoughts ran through Larry's head.

It felt like a switchboard gone berserk. *"False prophets, ungodly people, worshipers of evil, adversaries, satanic forces..."* But who were they, and how could they be stopped? His son was dead. But why? It didn't make any sense. His wife was too. Did she know something? If so maybe, just maybe it all made sense. He continued reading...

2nd Corinthians 11:14; *"Satan and his minions disguise themselves in cloaks of righteousness. Their end will correspond to their deeds."*

In the book of Revelation June had highlighted, *"The beast will make war on those who give testimony, to conquer and kill them all."*

Also in Revelation, 16:14; *"Demonic spirits go abroad, to assemble the kings of the world for battle."*

The more Larry read the clearer it became. There were forces at work. Evil forces, all hellbent on destroying all that man had become. Satanist who would never give up. Not without accomplishing their evil agenda. And they had to be stopped.

When Larry got to the end of the Book of Revelation he noticed June had scribbled something at the bottom of the page. Much of what was written was indecipherable gibberish. Incoherent thoughts and unfinished sentences he could barely make out. She'd written things like, *"Elect of the inner circle, Kabbalism is the key, Ancient Adepts, Dual Doctrines."*

The scribbled half statements didn't make much sense. Who the hell was the elect of the inner circle? What was Kabbalism? The Ancient who?

The last page of June's bible had been a blank page until she filled it in with more gibberish. At the very top of the page she'd written an interesting quote. *"Many are called...Some are chosen."* Satanael, the Elder...

Was that supposed to be scriptural? Who the hell was Satanael, the Elder?

Directly below this odd statement was a number of dates, followed by a series of words...all of them written in Latin. Larry recalled that his wife had majored in foreign languages back at Florida Southern University. He studied the dates one by one, trying to understand the puzzle. Piecing it together one date at a time.

1128 - initium est 1312 - terminus
18/03/1314 - auto da fe'

Here the dates were separated by a predicate his wife had written before continuing. This predicate was also in Latin.

UT SUB TERA - REVERTETUR IN TERRUM - UNUM
(Go underground - Return to earth - Become one)

Following this were more dates:

1641 - rosa o 1717 - London
01/05/1776 13-33-300
1813 - subcinctus imperium 15/03/1842 - JS primo a parte
1859 - P traditi sumus in direptionem

Following these dates was a long list of names. Some of them Larry recognized. Some he didn't.

NOMINA LAUDIS

Jacques de Molay, Christian Rosenkreuz, Benjamin Franklin, Adam Weishaupt, Joseph Smith, Albert Pike, John D Rockefeller, Winston Churchill, George Bush

One final name appeared on the list. Why it was there Larry could not understand. It didn't make any sense to him. Why would his wife add this name to that list?

And who was it you might ask?

None other than Elliot Prince. Now what in the world could possibly connect him... to them?

June had insisted Elliot Prince was evil. She'd actually referred to him as satanic. And she was adamant he had killed their son. When June told her husband she was certain the CEO of Head-Hunter Records was involved he'd ignored her.

Larry had befriended the man...and his cohorts. He'd actually arranged a golf outing for them. He'd invited them to attend his son's funeral. Larry had pranced around like a goddamn jackass while those bastards laughed at him behind his back.

But they say he who laughs last, laughs best!

AN AMERICAN IDOL
The Illuminate Conspiracy

CHAPTER TWENTY-TWO

Larry had been quite busy since moving to Naples. He'd gone there to work on Richard Tejada's presidential campaign and the job consumed most of his time. He felt truly fortunate to have been befriended by such a vibrant personality. The fact the lieutenant governor let Larry stay in his house made his transition from middle aged multimillionaire to middle class day planner a lot more palatable.

No one had to know he was a hired hand. Larry could drive through town in his classic red corvette with his head held high. Though a small city (population 21,683) Naples, Florida has the second highest proportion of millionaires per capita in the United States. It also boasts eighty golf courses. A good thing, since one of Larry's most important duties is accompanying his employer on the greens.

As Richard Tejada's golf partner Larry got to meet many of Naples most notable citizens. Among them former astronaut Buzz Aldrin, NBA superstar Larry Bird, Mike Ditka of the Chicago Bears, and Dick Gephardt, the former Leader of the House of Representatives. Several of them became huge financial supporters of the Tejada presidential campaign.

Now here he was sitting at a fancy Moroccan style open air terrace in downtown Los Angeles enjoying a mojito with the person who could very well be the next President of the United States. As a paying guest at the Luxe Hotel City Center Larry was welcome to enjoy the hotel's luxurious embellishments, and all courtesy of Head-Hunter Media Group. His meals, transportation, even his bar tab were all included.

The Luxe City Center is directly across the street from the NOKIA Theatre, the site of this years Rock and Roll Hall of Fame induction ceremony. Though considered a boutique hotel the amenities at The Luxe rival many of the more upscale hotels located along Sunset Boulevard and Rodeo Drive.

Larry had come prepared for the occasion. He'd done a whole lot of research since discovering his wife's bible in that box at the storage facility. Especially concerning the notes she'd scribbled down in it.

After getting down on his hands and knees at that motel in New Smyrna Beach and accepting Jesus Christ as his personal savior Larry had prayed for a revelation of his own. If Elliot Prince was somehow responsible for his son's death there would be hell to pay...

In the weeks and months leading up to the induction ceremony Larry had managed to keep a low profile. He would have liked to talk to his boss about his findings but he knew Tejada was tight with The Prince. Truth is Larry wondered if his employer might be involved in some way. He wondered why Tejada was the beneficiary of Prince's good will? For that matter what was the lieutenant governor's connection with Stanton Price. After all it was Stanton Price, Jr. that his wife had tried to assassinate that day.

He'd always found it odd the way both Prince and Tejada so readily submitted to the California real estate developer. After all, the two men appeared to be his superior, at least career wise. Why would the CEO of the most successful music and entertainment empire in the world and a future candidate for President of the United States cater to Stanton Price, Jr? Even if he was rich...

Larry had delved into the scriptures. He'd also used an online language translator to familiarize himself with both Latin and Greek. Though most of his wife's notes were indecipherable Larry was able to decode some of it. What he discovered was extremely troubling.

He started with the dates June had annotated on the last page of her bible. Larry found that the year 1128 AD corresponded with the year a British religious order of knights was granted a papal sanction by Pope Honorius II. The order's stated mission had been to protect pilgrims traveling to and from the Holy Land during the crusades.

Larry also learned that the King of Jerusalem had granted the British knights quarters in his palace, which had been built on the original site of King Solomon's Temple. Because of this the group became known as The Knights of the Temple. He also discovered these Temple Knights went on to win favor with European royalty. They did this by successfully conquering Muslim strongholds in the Middle East. The Knights of the Temple soon became the leading recruiters of European armies sent to battle in the crusades.

The Knights of the Temple received generous donations from the wealthy pilgrims they protected. In time these knights would come to accumulated a great deal of wealth. Enough in fact to purchase valuable properties throughout the European continent.

In 1312 AD the order was suddenly abolished. Pope Clement V discovered their ranks had been corrupted by the very Gnostics they were sent to convert. Over the years many of the Temple Knights had been strongly influenced by Palestinian sects practicing occultism. These truths were confirmed by The Templars Grand Master, Jacques de Molay, during a Papal tribunal held in Paris.

De Molay, along with his three highest ranking officers, had been summoned to Paris to answer rumors circulating throughout Europe that The Knights of the Temple were guilty of committing gross heresy. On the eighteenth day of March, 1314, De Molay was burned alive at the stake after openly confessing he'd practiced satanical worship with other members of his order. This particular form of justice became known as Auto de Fe, meaning Act of Faith, as penance for sins against God.

Word spread throughout the continent that The Temple Knights had become masters of deception, and that they engaged in horrific diabolical atrocities while publicly appearing to serve Christ. Members of the Order were hunted down and publicly forced to confess their sins. Many admitted partaking in phallicism and Satanism, desecrating the crucifix, revering the false idol Baphomet, and engaging in sodomy and other various unnatural vices. They also suffered Auto de Fe for their atrocities.

Further research showed some of the Temple Knights escaped justice by finding refuge in Portugal under King Dinis II. He in essence became their protector. Larry discovered that eventually most of the property these knights owned was confiscated. Still those who survived the inquisition remained influential. The Order had been made up noblemen and aristocrats. Men of renown who'd proven their muster in battle. They continued to operate under other headings, governed by men using fictitious names to protect their identity.

The surviving Templars eventually founded a secret organization called Ancient Adepts of the Rose Cross. The Adepts continued to pursue their belief in the occult, practicing the same ritualistic ceremonies they'd engaged in back in Jerusalem. They operated clandestinely for several centuries.

One day it was decided that it was time to find out how the public would respond to their occultist philosophies. To do so they would need to remain anonymous. The Order had long ago learned public perception could bring dire consequences. It was obvious they couldn't reveal their true identity as Templars. They determined the best way to accomplish their agenda was to invent a fictitious character. Hence the appearance of a someone named Christian Rosenkreutz.

The year was 1641. A tale was formulated telling the exploits of this Rosenkreutz fellow. The man had presumedly traveled to the Middle East to study the mystics. Rosenkruetz' surname was cleverly conceived by combining the name of the Templar's new Order, The Rose Cross. Given the title 'Fama Fraternis,' this fictitious biography elaborated on how Christian Rosenkreutz came to learn the wonders of mysticism from the great masters of eastern philosophy, and how he returned to Europe in a state of perpetual enlightenment.

The book was accepted as the gospel truth by most of the people who read it. Christian Rosenkreutz himself was much sought after by those who wished to learn more about eastern mysticism. Of course no one was ever able to locate the fictional man. But that didn't stop a number of societies from springing up all throughout Europe, all of them claiming to possess Christian Rosenkreutz' secrets of enlightenment.

Because of the success of that book The Ancient Adepts of the Rose Cross were able to come out of the shadows. They used yet another pseudonym, 'The Rosicrucian Society,' again a play on words, to hide behind the fictional Christian Rosenkreutz character. The Ancient Adepts discovered European society had become much more lenient to their beliefs. Times had changed. Though massively powerful the Roman Catholic Church no longer ruled Europe with an iron fist. In fact a keen interest in eastern mysticism soon spread throughout the continent. So much so The Rosicrucians began publicly recruiting members in an effort to gain fortune and further their public acceptance.

June had written the date 1717 in her bible. When Larry typed it into his laptop he found the date corresponded with the forming of yet another new fraternal order, this one known as The Freemasons. The Fraternal Order of Freemasons was a society of free thinking men who saw themselves as self governing, and therefore without the need for governmental intervention or church rule. They believed all men were, in their souls, good and just.

The Masonic message rang true in the hearts of many. By the end of the eighteenth century the Freemasons became firmly established as an organization known for their good works and benevolence towards their fellow man. Membership skyrocketed.

What June was able to see, though it wasn't clearly spelled out, was that the Rosicrucians had been the forebears of the Freemason movement from the outset. The entire idea being a diabolical scheme to hide the Templars existence from those who'd see them exposed for what they really were. Satanic worshipers of Luciferian doctrine dedicated to creating a New World Order.

Like their predecessors before them Freemasons used deception to mask their true identity. The lie begun during the crusades in the fourteenth century was being perpetuated in present day Europe. Whilst thousands of dedicated and honorable men carried out the facade for which they had been recruited the true goals of the Masonic hierarchy was being carried out by the men who'd originally put the wheels in motion. The Ancient Adepts of the Rose Cross... The Knights Templar.

The forebears of the Masonic movement intended to hide the true nature of their existence from the majority of its members. There was no need to reveal Templar secrets to men who lacked the intelligence and vision to implement them. They would establish a pyramid of sorts, consisting of thirty-three degrees of training. Each level would bring one a step closer to their destiny. Only those hand selected would make it to the inner circle.

On the 1st of May, 1776 a new ultra secret society was founded within the hierarchy of the Freemason organization. The Illuminati's mission was to shine the light of truth on man's true destiny and by doing so secure Satanael's rightful place on his throne. This would be accomplished by overthrowing all civil authority and abolishing Christianity.

The original make up of the Illuminati consisted of three hundred and forty-six men, all selected from a pool of upper level Freemasons. Thirteen of them, chosen as Druids, were collectively known as 'The Council of Thirteen.' A sub council of thirty-three men was made up from those who had earned all thirty-two levels of their Masonic degrees. They were called 'The Council of 33.' A second sub council consisted of the remaining three-hundred men, many of whom came from the wealthiest dynasties on the continent. The person chosen to lead this ultra secret society would come from within 'The Council of Thirteen.' He'd be known as 'Grand Pindar.'

The first to be chosen as Illuminati Grand Pindar was a man named Albert Weishaupt. Weishaupt, who happened to be a German Jew, was ironically an expert on Canon law. He actually assisted 'The Society of Jesus,' (better known today as the Jesuits) when called upon to help them interpret Canon law. Weishaupt's ability to deceive the leadership of Europe's Christian churches is a testament to his satanical genius.

During his tenure Albert Weishaupt was able to to gain ecumenical support for the Freemason movement. His largest contribution to the Illuminati however was his ability to secure a financial alliance with the international banking consortium headed by the Rothschild family. That alliance provided the Freemason organization with the ability to carry out its long range plans, and restored the fraternal order's financial prominence once held by the Knights Templar.

With the financial backing of the Rothschilds the Illuminati was able to draw men of royal and noble title into its domain. This only added to the momentum of the Freemason movement. It should be noted that at the time Weishaupt forged this alliance the Rothschild family was the richest family on earth. Wealthier even than the British government itself. It was in fact the Rothschild family who financed the Napoleonic Wars, which of course culminated with Napoleon's defeat to the British at Waterloo. Interestingly, the Napoleonic Wars also brought an end to the Holy Roman Empire, which itself had its origins in the middle ages.

Further research told Larry the Freemasons moved their central core of operations to the United States in 1813. Its leaders recognized the young swiftly growing country would soon dominate its European brethren politically, financially, and spiritually. It was clear America would become a world power. If the Adepts were going to be successful they'd have to control the masses where they lived.

Many of America's founding fathers were Freemasons, though most remained in the lower degrees of their training. Few could have known the true nature of the organization they'd joined. Namely Occultism, Satanic worship, and world dominance. Deception was the key. Let the foolish frolic around serving their fellow man while the enlightened few handle the internal affairs of the master. And one way they could continue the deception and keep Christians from coming together was by inspiring the formation of Christian religious cults. Freemasons in hierarchical positions of power helped spread the rise of Christian Science, Unitarianism, and Jehovah's Witness. All these cults have resulted in people being subtly directed away from the truth of Jesus Christ.

The biggest cult of them all was started by a man named Joseph Smith. Smith played right into the hands of The Ancient Adepts when he published his book of Mormon in 1830. Most of his followers don't know that twelve years after publishing that book Joseph Smith became a member of the Fraternal Order of Freemasons. On March 15, 1842 Smith earned his initial degree in Freemasonry. Just one day later he was named a Master Mason by leaders of the Freemason organization. One hand washes the other does it not?

Six weeks after Joseph Smith earned his sublime degree he was back in Salt Lake City teaching the 'revelations' shown him by Freemason leadership to his Mormon underlings, all the while claiming they'd been revealed to him by God. Anyone who cares to look will see the obvious connection between Mormonism and Freemasonry. The two organizations share similar symbolism, similar religious rituals, and similar secret doctrine.

In the year 1859 Freemasonry was 'Illuminized'. That's the year a man named Albert Pike was chosen as Sovereign Grand Master. Pike restructured the brotherhood in an effort to force it back onto the path for which it was formed. That being to prepare the way for Satanael, the Elder.

Albert Pike had a gift for being able to captivate an audience with his oratorical skills. People would listen to him for hours on end, thinking they'd been in the presence of greatness. He was fluent in over a dozen languages, and wasn't shy about showing it. Pike was also an expert on the occult and eastern mysticism. He wrote dozens of books on the subject, some of which became Masonic classics.

His work 'The Book of Apadno' contains prophesies about the reign of the anti-Christ, as told from a satanic point of view. Another one of his works would become what some in the movement describe as the Freemason bible. 'Morals and Dogma of the Ancient Adepts' is considered Albert Pike's most prominent book.

What set Pike apart from his fellow Adepts was his insistence that a Freemason's true calling be revealed to him earlier in his training. He believed no enlightened man could hear the truth and not recognize the obvious. Prior to Pike's ascension to the office of Sovereign Grand Master only someone who'd earned all thirty-two Masonic degrees was allowed into the inner circle. Upon reaching that distinction the member was formerly introduced to Luciferic doctrine. He discovered the true nature of his calling.

But Pike lowered that requirement. He determined that a Freemason was ready for enlightenment upon completion of only his thirteenth degree of training. Pike's reasoning was sound. The first twelve degrees of Freemasonry serve as a conditioning school, preparing a candidate for the ultimate acceptance of Luciferic initiation. Pike figured any member making it that far in his training had already been practicing occultism anyway. It just wasn't blatant.

Some in the inner circle feared members who hadn't fulfilled their training might reject the truth. Pike believed the opposite would happen. He believed those who'd gotten that far already suspected the true nature of their calling. Confirming it would make them feel included. If the organization were going to move forward it needed soldiers dedicated to the cause. And an enlightened man was more valuable to the overall success of the movement than one still in the dark. With the Freemason's web of deception soundly supported by the vast majority squandering in lower level degrees the Adepts could carry out their plan without trepidation.

It was the perfect ploy. Who would ever believe Freemasonry was a massive conspiracy to usher in a New World Order? No one! The Ancient Adepts would fulfill their destiny and become Masters of the Universe. One ruled by a single centralized government, with but one agenda. One small step for man would be one giant leap for mankind…

AN AMERICAN IDOL
The Illuminati Conspiracy

CHAPTER TWENTY-THREE

When I say Larry London came prepared I mean he fully intended to finish what his dead wife had started six years before. June had been right all along. His research confirmed it. Their son had been murdered by an exclusive group of Satan worshipping occultist.

Several other very well known, very successful entertainers had met similar fates in recent years. Their deaths were all over the news when they happened. A double Oscar winning actress was found dead in her Pacific Palisades mansion with her belly sliced open. It was widely reported she was six months pregnant and rumor had it when the police found her the unborn fetus was missing. Another very successful fella, a singer like Jeremy London, was electrocuted while performing in concert. The culprit was said to be an improperly grounded microphone stand.

Healthy, successful, presumedly happy people whose lives ended quite unexpectedly. What do you suppose they had done to cause their demise? Not play along perhaps?

These type of things had to be stopped. If it was anywhere near as widespread and demonic as Larry feared he couldn't depend on the local authorities for help. For all he knew they were part of it. No, he'd have to take matters into his own hands. Thanks to his wife's clues Larry knew exactly who it was he was fighting.

He'd wanted to bring his .357 magnum with him. The same gun June had snuck into her bag before Jeremy's funeral that day. The thirty-eight caliber revolver packed enough fire power to fulfill the requirements of his mission and held enough casings to ensure no one would be left standing who shouldn't be. Besides, it seemed appropriate under the circumstances. Despite the emotional ties he chose not to.

He and Richard Tejada had been booked on an early departing red eye out of Ft Myers. Bringing a handgun would have invited two things Larry was hoping to avoid. Paperwork and questions. First off, airline security would check to ensure all FAA regulations had been adhered to. Larry would be required to fill out a shit load of documentation, and when he arrived in California the authorities would have to be notified. Secondly Tejada would be sure to find out. Larry needed to avoid any mention he was packing heat.

There'd be no reason for him to bring a gun. What was he going to do, go target shooting on Santa Monica Boulevard? Tejada knew Larry was a recreational shooter, but he'd be suspicious. Either that or he'd think he was crazy. In any case Larry couldn't take the chance Elliot Prince might find out.

He came to California with a plan. Larry had scoped everything out in advance. As exclusive as his hotel was it was within ten minutes walking distance of a downtrodden neighborhood known as 'The Nickel.'

The Nickel is how locals refer to a five block section of Fifth Street just east of downtown L.A. It is bound by Angeles Street to the west and San Pedro to the east. Once the sun sets The Nickel is overrun by a pretty seedy collection of aging prostitutes, heroin addicts, pedophiles, and homeless war veterans seeking refuge from the battleground that is their life. It's a place where a man with cash in his wallet can buy anything from a slightly used wedding ring to a still smoking Israeli Uzi.

After checking into the hotel Larry told Tejada he was going to unpack his bag then go for a jog. He invited the portly politician to join him, knowing full well he wouldn't. With a three hour lag time due to the time zone changes Larry figured he had plenty of time to take care of business.

When Larry London walked out of The Luxe Hotel twenty minutes later he looked like a man on a mission. He turned left and headed down South Figueroa Street. When he got to Fifth Street he took a right. You'd have thought he'd been there all his life.

San Julian Park, aka: 'Thieves Corner,' sits at the intersection of San Julian and Fifth Street, right in the heart of The Nickel. The gates are locked at night to keep the homeless out. During the day the green area is home to dozens. The park is a mecca for small time crack dealers and petty thieves selling their wares. Any experienced shopper can get himself a used iphone for ten bucks. A used iPod for thirty. An unregistered handgun might set you back a cool hundred.

Entering the park Larry looked like a fish out of water. His navy blue polyester jogging outfit and white as snow running shoes made him so. Everyone else was wearing a haphazard array of ill fitting, heavily soiled work pants, blue jeans, sweatshirts, and parkas. A few sported weather beaten LA Dodgers baseball caps.

Most everyone was lying on the grass behind the gated green iron fence. It was nearly impossible to tell the women from the men, but Larry thought there were a few. No one really bothered anyone else. You sensed it was a community. Some people enjoyed the comfort of a cardboard bed. Others rested their heads on pillows made of rolled up editions of the L.A. Times or pieces of styrofoam packing material salvaged from nearby dumpsters.

Larry hadn't been there two minutes when he was approached by an old black man with an unsanitary looking scarf wrapped around his neck. The black marketeer pulled up the sleeve of the ragged jacket he was wearing to reveal half a dozen watches ticking away on his arm. Larry shook his head no to indicate he wasn't in the market, then headed for the other end of the park.

An attractive, seemingly out of place young woman was standing by herself slowly rocking a powder blue baby stroller. She was wearing camouflage cargo pants and a pink LA Clippers sweatshirt cut off at the midriff. She wore long dangling silver earrings, which glistened in the morning sun. After a few minutes the woman glanced over at Larry, then motioned for him to look inside the stroller. When he did she reached down and pulled back a hand knitted baby blanket. Larry London couldn't believe his eyes, or his luck.

Coddled beneath the blanket was a Smith and Wesson 38 special identical to the one he owned back home. Larry slowly looked up at the young woman, who'd subtly put her index finger to her lips to caution him. She motioned for him to follow her, then pushed her stroller through the green iron gate and down Fifth Street.

About half way down the block was a dingy coffee shop. A sign in the window informed passersby that the restrooms were for PAYING CUSTOMERS ONLY. The woman with the baby stroller went inside. When Larry walked in a moment later the young woman was sitting at a table near the back of the coffee shop nonchalantly rocking her stroller back and forth. Larry went to the counter and ordered two coffees, then joined her.

"So tell me young lady. How did you know I was looking for that particular weapon," he asked as he set the two coffees down. *"Are you a cop? Please don't tell me you are working undercover? You're obviously not homeless..."*

Without giving the thoroughly inexperienced arms dealer a chance to answer Larry bellowed out, *"Look, I'm a licensed gun owner, lady. I collect handguns as a hobby. I assure you I am not a criminal. Don't arrest me!"*

"I saw you," she replied. *"In my dream."*

"Excuse me," Larry replied incredulously.

"I know that must sound crazy, but it's true," the woman insisted. *"I had this dream the other night. My spirit guide visited me. He told me I would meet someone who was on a sacred mission. That this person was going to save mankind. My spirit guide said he was going to stop Evil before it destroyed the world. You must believe me... There's no way in hell I could make this up."*

Incredibly, Larry did! After reading his dead wife's annotations and discovering the truth of Satan's plan for mankind. After asking God to give him a revelation, Larry did believe her. If he had any doubts prior to today they were gone now. Talk about confirmation.

The young woman continued. *"Here's the thing, Mister. I work for a gun dealer over in Montecito. Half the population of Los Angeles owns a weapon these days. In my dream my spirit guide described this type gun to me. Then low and behold it came into the shop. Out of the blue someone wanted to sell it. In my dream my spirit guide told me to bring it down to 'The Nickel.' He said I would meet someone dressed just like you. I thought the whole thing was crazy but... I'm a very spiritual person as you can plainly see. This is not the first time he has used me."*

Larry thought about it for a moment. The whole thing was crazy, but these were crazy times. He suggested the woman take her stroller and go into the ladies room. He would join her there when the coast was clear and they'd make the exchange.

As the young woman got up to leave Larry extended his hand and introduced himself. The woman took it, then leaned forward and whispered, *"I'm Felecia."* Then she turned and pushed her stroller towards the ladies rest room.

Just as Larry was about to make his move some lady pushed past him and walked into the ladies room. A moment later she came back out muttering something about a baby stroller being in the way so she couldn't get to the toilet. She kept on walking so Larry looked around then ducked into the ladies room to make the deal. But no one was in there. The stroller was. Its pink blanket was pulled all the way up. Larry reached under the blanket and felt around for the gun. It was heavy in his hand as he lifted it out of the stroller and stuffed it under his jacket. *"What the hell,"* he said aloud, more confused than ever.

Larry cursed to himself as he made his way to the front of the coffee shop and out the front door. Why hadn't he worn something more suitably to concealing a weapon in... Dumb Ass. He double timed it back up Fifth Street. When he reached South Figueroa he slowed his pace a bit, sweat running down his forehead. He stopped for a second to use the sleeve of his jacket to wipe it away.

That's when he became cognizant of the fact he was being followed. He turned to see an LAPD patrol car inching its way toward him. Moments later a police officer rolled his car window down and told him to hold up a minute.

Larry was just one inner city block from freedom. He considered making a run for it but he knew that would be a mistake. The last thing he needed was a nasty scene with the police right outside the entrance to his hotel. *"Is everything okay, Officer,"* Larry asked? *"Did I jaywalk? Sorry, I'm a visitor. I'm staying at The Luxe just down the street."*

"Yeah, you're okay," the officer responded. *"Just making a routine stop. I noticed you was down at 'The Nickel' awhile back. That's a dangerous neighborhood, Friend. You got business down there?"*

Rather than panic Larry felt a calmness come over him. He chuckled at his predicament, then explained how he'd gone out for a morning jog and mistakenly ended up down in Skid Row. *"I've never seen so many homeless people in my life, poor Son's a Bitch's."*

The cop shook his head in agreement. *"We got a call from one of the establishments down on Fifth. Some woman was seen pushing a baby stroller into one of the coffee shops down there. Evidently she run off and left the stroller sitting in the ladies room. The owner of the place thought she abandoned her baby or something but the stroller was empty. The Nickel ain't no place for a child anyway. You happen to see anything while you was out jogging?"*

"No," Larry responded. *"Not a thing."*

The officer tipped his cap and started back to his car, then hesitated.

Larry saw the question in the cop's eyes before he even asked it. *"What's that you got under your jacket, Sir?"*

OH FUCK! What to do now? How the hell does someone hide a .357 magnum from a suspicious police officer? *"Believe it or not it's a bible,"* Larry laughingly answered, not really sure where the hell the explanation came from. *"I picked it up at a shop down in The Nickel. Thought I'd do a little souvenir shopping. It's just easier to carry it like this... I got no pockets,"* he shrugged.

The cop laughed. *"You bought a bible in Skid Row... That's a good one, Man. Remember to say a little prayer for them poor lost souls, okay Bro."*

"Will do," Larry answered. *"As a matter of fact I'm going to say a little prayer for the entire city of Los Angeles tonight. After all it is the City of Angels, is it not?"*

With that the cop got back in his patrol car. He checked his mirrors than did a U-turn and headed back the way he came. Larry let out a huge sigh of relief. He took a moment to thank God then double timed it back to his room.

AN AMERICAN IDOL

The Illuminati Conspiracy

CHAPTER TWENTY-FOUR

Larry's plan was coming together like a charm. The incident with that cop could have really been disastrous. The way it turned out only confirmed his belief that this mission was divinely inspired.

He would have thought the young woman in the coffee shop was really weird, but he'd been married to someone who used to talk to God when she was alive. Larry used to listen to his wife having conversations with God himself through the bedroom door. Not praying, mind you... Having one on one conversations. Of course back then he thought she was crazy as a loon. The only voice he ever heard was hers.

Larry remembered the woman saying her name was Felecia, and that she worked for a gun dealer over in Montecito. She had told him she was being lead to him by some sort of spirit guide. That didn't necessarily equate to God. It sounded more like an Indian medicine man. Perhaps Felecia was American Indian? There are over fifty Native American tribes in California.

The way she just disappeared into thin air was really strange. There had been a small window in that ladies restroom but it was way too small for an adult to fit through. There was no sense dwelling on that now. What was, was... Larry figured if he somehow managed to survived this ordeal he'd look her up when it was all over. And that was a big IF...

The director of the Hall of Fame ceremony had scheduled an early afternoon walk through for today. Those appearing on stage were required to be there so that camera angles and lighting could be determined, as well as any questions addressed. Larry arrived just as the director's assistant was about to go over the program with everyone. Elliot Prince wasn't there, but no one seemed to notice.

Larry was told he'd be called up to the stage from his seat, which was front row center, after his son's name was announced. Elliot Prince would already be on stage, having entered from the wings. Each of them would have two minutes to talk about Jeremy and what he meant to the music industry, as well as to them personally.

A short film about Jeremy's life and accomplishments would be shown on a large screen behind them. It would highlight his winning the American Idol competition, receiving his first platinum record, and being presented his first Grammy Award. A clip of Jeremy's still talked about performance during the Super Bowl half-time show would then be shown using screenX technology.

The technology provides viewers with a panoramic two hundred and seventy degree experience by projecting the film onto the side walls of an auditorium as well as improving the surround sound effects. The film tribute will end with a segment filmed in black and white. It will show the Florida sun setting over Jeremy London's headstone. His mother's grave marker will be visible to the audience just to the left of her famous son's but there will be no verbal recognition.

Not on the program was Elliot Prince's plan to invite Richard Tejada to the stage. The presidential candidate wouldn't get any mic time, but his face would be seen by millions around the world. On his lapel will be a large Eye of Providence pin. Classic Illuminati subliminal messaging. Larry London will have no idea that little scenario is taking place.

The walk through played right into Larry's plan. Trying to sneak his weapon into the NOKIA Theatre as everyone is showing up would be extremely risky. Most likely everyone attending would have to pass through a metal detector before gaining access to the theatre. It's altogether possible they might even be frisked.

Security would be tight at any event attended by Hollywood royalty, and this was definitely an event...But thanks to the early afternoon walk through Larry was handed a golden opportunity to get his gun inside the theatre before security was set up. He just walked in and identified who he was and they let him pass on through.

He and Richard Tejada were scheduled to meet up with The Prince and Stanton Price in the VIP lounge an hour before the ceremony was to begin tonight. They'd have a drink and get reacquainted before taking their seats. Upon arriving at the theatre this afternoon for the walk through Larry visited the VIP lounge to scope it out. No one was there but the doors were open. He noticed there was a mens restroom just across from the VIP lounge. It was the perfect spot to hide his Smith & Wesson revolver. He'd have no problem retrieving it before the show started tonight.

Once back at the hotel Larry made his way to the outdoor terrace. Richard Tejada was there waiting for him. The two ordered a round of drinks and checked out the sights. Women were everywhere. This event brought out some of the highest class hookers in L.A. *"So did you get your morning jog in,"* Richard Tejada asked his once wealthy employee. In truth he thought the man a fool, but he'd been instructed to keep him close. Larry London had been the perfect patsy. He stood around like a fucking puppy on a leash as his son and wife were eliminated from the picture. Then he went and let a Goddamn gold digger rob him of everything his son had left him. As far as he was concerned the man was a fucking idiot.

"Yes, I did," Larry answered. *"Ended up on Skid Row somehow. Let me tell you it's unbelievable down there, Boss. Hobo's and drug addicts strung out like birds on a wire. Sad really. Even saw a few homeless war veterans. A couple of them was still wearing their fucking uniforms. Sad part is the fucking Taliban's still in control. They're still growing poppies, and still supplying the cartels."*

"The world is way to fucking overpopulated," Tejada responded. *"It was never meant to be this crowded. Maybe we can do something about that when we get in the white house. I'll make it a priority."*

Changing the subject the presidential hopeful suggested they invite a few of the ladies that were congregating on the terrace over for a drink. Larry shrugged his shoulders as if he weren't really interested. He asked his boss if Elliot Prince was going to be joining them for a drink.

He wasn't. The Prince had gone to visit Stanton Price Jr. at his place in La Jolla. They were planning to arrive in plenty of time for the ceremony. Flying over in Stanton's helicopter.

The remainder of the afternoon was spent downing Mojitos and eyeballing women. Larry was cautious not to overindulge. A few drinks would provide him some liquid encouragement but he needed to have his wits about him if he was going to pull his plan off without a hitch.

Tejada on the other hand drank like a damn fish. Outside the State of Florida he was still relatively unknown so he could let his hair down. That would change once the presidential hopeful won the primary. The more Mojitos Richard Tejada downed the more loquacious he became. He ended up inviting one of the 'ladies' on the terrace to join them for a drink, then spent the next hour bragging to her about his exploits as Lieutenant-Governor. He insisted he was a shoo in to win the California primary. To quote him, *"It was a done deal."*

Larry pressed Tejada on how that had been accomplished. Had the man been sober he might have suspected something, but he wasn't. So the words just spewed from his mouth like vomit.

"IF THEY WANT ME TO WIN, I'LL WIN. PERIOD! You don't really think I play the motley fool because I like to do you Larry? It's the price you pay if you want to get to the top of the mountain. You know that for Christ sake. Look at your Goddamn kid. You don't think Jeremy became the worlds most famous rock star on his own, do you? Don't get me wrong, the kid was good. Damn good… But so are a lot of singers. Jesus, Man... THEY DECIDE WHO RIDES THE BULL, AND THEY DECIDE WHO GETS BUCKED OFF. Everyone in this FUCKING burg knows that, Larry. Time for you to wake the fuck up… Buddy Boy."

Larry downplayed the fat fucker's comments. He thanked the young lady who'd graced their cabana for coming and promised her they would try to hook up with her later that evening after his friend slept it off. Then he put his arm around Richard Tejada's waist and helped him to his room.

Richard Tejada was staying in a penthouse suite. A candidate for the presidency of the United States can't be expected to stay in a mere hotel room. On the elevator ride up Larry tried to garner more information from his inebriated employer. Who the hell was this THEY he kept talking about? After making sure Tejada was safe in his bed Larry went back to his own room. He pulled the window curtain closed and fluffed his pillow, then set his alarm for 6:30. He needed to be across the street before 8:00. It was going to be an eventful night.

AN AMERICAN IDOL
The Illuminati Conspiracy

CHAPTER TWENTY-FIVE

Larry looked spectacular in the tuxedo he'd purchased for the event. It was traditional black on black, with a crisp white Milani shirt and a black clip on bow-tie. He'd cleverly hand sewn a custom made holster inside the coat's silk lining.

On Elliot Prince's insistence Larry was drinking something called a 'Kinky Boots' cocktail. Stanton Price, Jr. was there too. Both men were coaching him a little. The conversation centered around Stanton's suggestion that Larry be sure to thank the music industry for allowing his son the opportunity to make a difference. And of course Head-Hunter Records for signing him in the first place.

"When your kid first signed with Head-Hunter he was totally clueless," added The Prince. *"We molded him. Mention that, Larry. The crowd will eat it up..."* It was Elliot Prince's last piece of advice that stuck with Larry however. He'd said, *"Remember one thing, Larry... These are our people!"*

YOUR PEOPLE? Interesting concept, Mr. Prince... My son was one of YOUR PEOPLE... Look how well that turned out for him, so Larry thought. He'd really wanted to tell him that, but he didn't. Instead he put his personal feelings aside and thanked Elliot for his kind advice. After finishing his 'Kinky Boot' cocktail Larry excused himself, saying he needed to make a pit stop before the show started. *"A case of pre-speech jitters,"* he lied.

His weapon was right where he left it earlier that afternoon. Larry locked the stall door then reached down and removed the plastic liner from the waste basket. But before he was able to secure the gun someone came waltzing into the men's room to use the urinal. Larry took a seat and waited. Whoever it was didn't bother to wash his hands after taking a piss. So much for high society he thought to himself. When the coast was clear Larry resumed his preparations.

The Smith and Wesson revolver sat heavy in its makeshift holster. The extra weight forced Larry to alter his stance a bit in order to accommodate for it. After reassuring himself in the mirror he flushed the toilet and headed out. Destiny was waiting.

When Larry stepped off the elevator he was immediately star struck. The inferiority complex he thought he'd lost while walking through Skid Row that morning came rushing back with a vengeance. The lobby of the NOKIA Theatre was teaming with celebrity.

He'd just spent the last forty minutes upstairs hobnobbing with world renown musicians and record producers in the VIP lounge but this was where the action was. It wasn't just famous musicians either. Larry recognized Oscar winning actors and television stars. Even a few sports celebrities.

Larry actually got to speak with rock icon Joan Jett for a few moments. She and her band were scheduled to do a number on the show tonight. Supposedly a tribute to Jeremy. Joan told Larry she was a huge Jeremy London fan. She seemed much softer than Larry expected, given her public persona. Perhaps it was her age. We all tone it down a bit eventually.

There was a hum of excitement in the air as Larry made his way to his seat in the front row of the theatre. He was dead center to the stage. A few minutes after he sat down Elliot Prince and Stanton Price, Jr. arrived. Richard Tejada was nowhere to be found. While waiting for the festivities to begin Elliot leaned over and told Larry that the NOKIA Theatre was the site of the final round of American Idol the night his son was crowned. He seemed surprised to hear it. His reaction was a little off, considering.

Larry had forgotten that. After all it had been eight years ago. But when Elliot said it it came rushing back. All the old feelings did. The guilt he felt for being a failure. He had failed as a father. Failed as a husband. Failed as a business man. Failed as a fucking human being. Something sinister overtook Larry's body in that moment.

It started low where his ankles attached to his feet. Then it slowly crawled its way up his legs to his groin. The burning sensation continued its upward spiral, passing through Larry's bowels and into his chest. From there the fire ripped through his gullet before finally settling in his brain. It was not like anything he'd ever experienced before. Indescribable really. It was like a live wire. An impassioned impulse of unadulterated hatred that completely neutralized his other senses.

The man could neither hear nor speak. He could not see nor feel. It felt like every nerve in his body had been stimulated simultaneously.

Larry London had come to California with intent. His wife and son were dead, victims of a satanical force so powerful it couldn't be stopped by human hands alone. Larry had come to terms with his relationship with God. He'd accepted Christ as his personal savior and vowed to do whatever he could to slay The Beast. What he planned was premeditated to the nth degree. This however was different.

This was not premeditated. What he was experiencing in that moment was without forethought or reflection. What Larry experienced was total separation from whatever it was that made him human. In that moment he was void of compassion. Unable to feel remorse. Why he didn't pull out his gun right then and there and blow Elliot Prince's face off is anybody's guess.

The feeling dissipated with the on stage arrival of Grammy winning recording artist 'Sion's Crypt.' The heavy metal band seemed to beckon Larry's return to sanity with their hard driving beat. The band's sound, played against an audiovisual backdrop of American bombers dropping their payload on Japanese cities filled the auditorium.

When the band finished their number the lead singer made a beeline towards the edge of the stage. He looked straight at Larry, holding his gaze for what seemed like an eternity. The musician's bright blue eyes sat in deep pockets of thick black eye shadow. When he finally released his gaze the rocker turned his attention to Stanton Price, Jr.

Price was sitting two seats away. What happened next defied logic, and sent a chill down Larry London's spine. The singer's eyes took on a reptilian appearance, and the color changed from a beautiful bright blue to a murky green.

It happened so fast Larry wondered if he'd imagined it. The singer blinked and his eyes morphed into something resembling a lizards. Green globes with black vertical slits. He blinked again and they returned to normal. If that were all there was to it it would be one thing...but there was more!

When the singer released his gaze and moved on to Elliot Prince Larry turned to watch Stanton Price's reaction. He was shocked to see the man's eyes do the same fucking thing. He'd swear to it on a stack of bibles.

The show went on. A popular comedian was hosting, and he did a great job of keeping things rolling, making fun of some of the more famous celebrities seated towards the front. Especially the men. He referred to Elliot Prince as 'The Hunchback of Un-noble Fame.' He told Steven Tyler if he had been on the Titanic no one would have had to drown. They could have used his lips as giant life rafts. He made the same analogy about Jaylo's bottom, suggesting Titanic survivors could have hopped on board and paddled their way home. He volunteered to demonstrate if she would allow.

When it was Jeremy London's turn to be honored Joan Jett walked onto the stage. No band, just her alone. She stepped forward and took a bow. Larry sensed that her reverence was really directed at Stanton Price, Jr because she looked right at him as she bent over.

Then she backpedalled her way to the rear curtain where she froze. Suddenly a blinding flash went off and the black leather clad rocker broke into a tough as nails rendition of a little known 1970's rock song. Suzi Quatro's, 'Daytona Demon.'

As great as Joan Jett's performance was Larry thought it was marred by unnecessary props. The backdrop for the song was a realistic 3D image of Daytona Beach, complete with boardwalk and pier. The same pier Jeremy London supposedly hung himself from. Dozens of computer generated bathing beauties milled about in skimpy bikinis, seemingly within easy reach of the audience.

Because the song's lyrics equate fast raucous race cars with well endowed lovers several replicas roared out from the wings. The cars raced around two towers set up on either end of the stage. On closer inspection it was plain to see the towers resembled two giant phalluses.

As Joan was finishing her tribute to Jeremy a glistening black Pontiac Trans Am screeched to a halt right beside her. A big red six was painted on the hood of the car, with two more on either side door panel. In a subtle display of subliminal messaging an allegorical Eye of Providence symbol sat inside the circle of each six. Adding to the imagery was a white owl perched on the tail of each number six, subliminally meant to convey wisdom, knowledge, and enlightenment...

Joan Jett climbed up on the roof of the Trans Am then motioned for the driver to take a victory lap around the stage. He revved the automobile's four hundred cubic inch engine then tossed his famous passenger a tether line.

The sexy, leather clad rocker stood spread eagle on the roof of the car, her life seemingly dependent on holding that tether line tight. The driver sped off, completed a figure eight around the stage, then came to a halt dead center facing the audience.

The entire theatre burst into applause. Their enthusiastic accolades were cut short when a brilliant flash of light came crashing down from on high and the stage filled with dense white smoke.

When the smoke cleared the stage was void. A complete blank canvas. No shiny black Trans Am. No computer generated babes in bikinis. No subliminal symbolism. And no Joan Jett... It was a disappearing act worthy of David Copperfield. Every single person in the theatre stood in shock and awe.

Jeremy London's posthumous induction into the Rock and Roll Hall of Fame had to try and follow that. How could anyone expect to top it? Joan Jett had outdone herself. People would be talking about her performance forever. There may have been some younger viewers watching at home who weren't familiar with Joan and her band The Black Hearts. But they would be now!

Larry had been so captivated by Joan Jett's performance he never noticed Elliot Prince leave his seat, or Richard Tejada take it. Once the audience settled down a deep resounding voice came over the loud speakers. *"Ladies and gentlemen, please welcome Mr. Elliot Prince. Chairman of the board of Head-Hunter Media Group. Mr. Prince will be accepting the Rock and Roll Hall of Fame induction award for rock superstar Jeremy Tobias London."*

As The Prince made his way to the podium from behind a dark curtain at the rear of the stage he was met by a curvaceous young model holding a twenty inch tall trophy. The award depicted a female form made out of black onyx. She stood on a black granite base holding a gold record disc high above her head. This one had the name Jeremy Tobias London inscribed on it.

Elliot thanked everyone in attendance for their generous applause. Every single person in the theatre had risen at the mention of Jeremy London's name. That brought tears to Larry's eyes. His son was loved. In the short span of two years Jeremy had touched the hearts of America through his music. Touched the hearts of the entire world really. He made a difference to every person who bought his records or heard his songs. It had been six years, and he was truly missed. If only June could have been there...

The Prince played the crowd for all they were worth. He told them Jeremy London was in a better place now. That he'd paid his dues and joined the inner circle. He bragged about taking the youthful singer with so much raw talent and sculpting him into a superstar. Elliot suggested Jeremy had been like a son to him. He went so far as to suggest that on occasion he'd had to punish the boy. *"Spare the rod and spoil the child, like my mother used to say, bless her soul."*

Some in the audience, all too familiar with what had happened at Jeremy's funeral, gasped when Elliot laughed and said, *"I'm not so sure Jeremy London's mom would agree with that philosophy."*

Perhaps it was their reaction that inspired Elliot to get on with his acceptance speech. When he told the audience there was someone in the theatre he wanted them to meet Larry squirmed in anticipation. He had no idea The Prince was going to point his index finger at Richard Tejada and say, *"Get on up here, my friend."*

Tejada stood and adjusted his tuxedo before making his way to the stage. Once there the rotund politician smiled and waved to the somewhat confused crowd. Elliot told the audience Richard Tejada was the lieutenant-governor of Florida and that he was running for President of the United States. He reminded them that the California primaries were being held the following week. Then he looked straight into the television camera and announced, *"Richard Tejada is a great man, Folks. He is my friend, and he deserves your votes. C'mon America. Vote for Richard Tejada for President."*

The Prince wrapped his arm around the big politician's shoulder and spoke into the microphone. *"Are you a music lover, Sir"* he inquired? Tejada answered yes, he certainly was. *"And what type of music do you love, Sir,"* The Prince politely asked? Tejada answered that he loved rock and roll, of course. Then Elliot, knowing what a huge reaction his next question would bring said, "And who is your favorite rock and roll singer, candidate Tejada?" Richard Tejada laughed as he responded, *"Why Jeremy London, of course!"*

The audience loved it. The way the two men played off each other was kind of funny. You could tell they were buddies. Elliot turned to Tejada and laughingly said, *"May I ask you one more questIon, SIr? When you win the White House are you going to throw a great big party in the Rose Garden and invite all of us?"*

The crowd roared. Elliot Prince had done his job. Millions of people were now familiar with the name Richard Tejada. He was branded as being one cool dude right from the get go.

But what did that have to do with Jeremy London's induction into the Rock and Roll Hall of Fame? Absolutely nothing. It was nothing but a great big photo op...

Larry's nerves were frayed. He wanted to do what he'd come to do and get it over with. These people were evil, and he was the only one who seemed to understand that. He was on a mission from God. And he'd come with intent. The Prince was going down. A photo op? I'll give you a fucking photo op!

Elliot thanked Tejada for joining them on stage this evening, then he explained to the audience why he'd really invited the portly politician to come up. *"We have another very special guest with us this evening, ladies and gentlemen. Someone who happens to be employed by my friend, Richard Tejada. Richard was kind enough to give this man a job when he discovered he'd fallen upon hard times. I would like you all to stand and give a big Rock and Roll Hall of Fame welcome to my good friend and Jeremy Tobias London's father... Larry London!"*

Larry was perspiring profusely as he lifted himself from his seat and made his way to the stage. His .357 magnum tugged at his tuxedo jacket. His breathing became labored. He could hear the audience murmuring as he climbed the steps leading to the podium. As he took the last step up he stumbled momentarily, fortunately catching himself before falling flat on his face.

Once on the stage Larry realized they had turned the house lights up. He turned to see seven thousand people wildly applauding him. Some were close enough to recognize. Rock stars and musicians he'd grown up idolizing. Everyone was on their feet honoring the memory of his son.

And that's why he'd come. To honor the memory of his son. It was personal. No one would know the truth. The people applauding him had no idea who the small group of men who made them all rich were. Or that they were evil incarnate. Nor did they know that he was there to correct that.

By the time security could react it would be too late. Larry would have to be true in his aim. He didn't want any more innocent blood to be shed. There had been enough of that already. He looked down at Stanton Price, Jr. sitting alone in the middle of the first row. The two of them made eye contact. It was now or never...

AN AMERICAN IDOL
The Illuminati Conspiracy

CHAPTER TWENTY-SIX

Larry's first shot was dead on. He made sure The Prince knew what hit him. He made sure he saw the gun. When Larry pulled that Smith and Wesson out of his tuxedo jacket and pointed it at Elliot's head the man knew his number was up.

The hollow point bullets the woman with the baby stroller supplied with the weapon answered any lingering questions Elliot may have had. A hole the size of a quarter appeared in the space between the record producer's eye brows. Joan Jett could have driven her shiny black Trans Am through the size hole the bullet made as it exited the back of his head.

It was ironic that Elliot Prince ended up on his knees when he took his last breath. They say that it's never too late to bow to the Lord in prayer. A second later Larry took out his next target. He was glad Stanton Price, Jr. was sitting between two vacant seats when he fired because the man's brains ended up splattering across the blue velveteen upholstery of all three seats. If The Prince or Richard Tejata had been sitting in their seats they would be dripping brain matter and blood all over their fancy tuxedos. Imagine the dry cleaning bill.

Larry knew that Stanton Price, Jr. knew what was coming. He'd seen it written all over the bastard's face. They say a picture paints a thousand words. When the two of them made eye contact the moment was freeze framed in perpetuity. The two of them shared an entire conversation in the twinkling of an eye.

There is no freedom in deception. No honor. Truth is the only thing that will set you free. Stanton Price, Jr had worshipped The Greatest Deceiver of them all. The reality of it was that he himself had been deceived. But thanks to Larry London his eyes had now been opened. Larry made sure of it. The Grand Pindar of the Draco was now Illuminized. In fact against the dark background of the NOKIA Theatre one could see the illumination pouring through the large ragged hole in the middle of Stanton Price's head.

Five heartbeats. That's all it took. There was no shouting. There was no pleading. Larry London had made no threats. He'd made no demands. He'd simply drawn his weapon, taken aim, and fired. Larry had a lot of practice on the shooting range all those years ago. For most of the seven thousand in attendance who witnessed it the entire event seemed surreal. Other than a few people in the first few rows no one had even reacted really. Everyone just remained in their seats, frozen like cubes in a tray.

Richard Tejada stood six feet to Larry London's left. The fat former lieutenant-governor was too frightened to move. He'd arrived late for the ceremony because he'd gone back down to the hotel terrace and picked up that young hooker. After all nobody knew him out here. How he wished he'd remained in his penthouse suite now. Had she not been so orally talented he'd probably still be there...

Tejada soiled his pants. The man who assumed he was to be the next President of the United States was standing on a stage in front of seven thousand people and a national television audience with human waste dripping down his thighs. How becoming. Hail to the fucking chief.

Larry didn't shoot him though. He wasn't a threat. The poor fat prick was just a means to an end. His punishment was being exposed for the fool he was. What Larry found really frightening was that Richard Tejada very well could have been elected. It made him wonder who else had sat in the oval office and done EXACTLY what he was told?

Very few people had moved from their seats. Larry thought that odd. He'd once read this article about how people instinctively put themselves closer to danger out of curiosity. A house on fire for example, or slowing down on a busy highway to catch a glimpse of a just happened car wreck. He himself had gone outside in curiosity when a neighbor called to tell him there was a black bear wondering around in his backyard raiding his trash can.

Perhaps for those in the theatre it was like watching a movie. Let's all stick around and find out what happens next. Larry approached the podium and tapped the mic a few times to see if it was on, then he addressed the crowd. *"My name is Larry London, ladies and gentlemen. I am... Well... I was... Jeremy London's father."*

The theatre was deadly silent. Quiet as a funeral. The only sounds came from an occasional cough or someone shifting in their seat. Then Larry spoke;

"I want you all to know my son did not kill himself," Larry informed them. *"Jeremy was murdered. His mother knew it. She tried to tell me but I wouldn't listen. June tried to stop the men who murdered our son herself but she failed. The poor woman had no experience firing weapons you see."*

Larry began to weep. He laid his revolver down on the podium as he apologized for ruining everyone's evening. Then he picked up where he had left off. *"My wife was a Christian woman. She might pray you to death but she would never shoot an innocent man. They killed her before she could expose them."*

Larry turned to Richard Tejada. The man hadn't dared to move a muscle since the whole thing began. He suggested he go now. The now friendless fat politico waddled off the stage as fast as his soiled tuxedo would allow.

Alone now on the stage Larry walked over to where Elliot Prince was still kneeling in silent prayer. Then he shifted his gaze towards Stanton Price, Jr., whose body was slumped across his seat in the front row of the center section. He lifted his arms and pointed to them simultaneously as he announced to everyone in attendance, "ILLUMINATI"

****

It started with a single person. A lady high up in the balcony towards the back. She stood and applauded. Then a second. Then a third. Before Larry knew what hit him everyone in the theatre was on their feet. The applause was deafening. Their acclamation affirmed his determination to act. In that moment, on that stage, Larry London was, like his son before him, AN AMERICAN IDOL...

THE END

AN AMERICAN IDOL
The Illuminati Conspiracy

EPILOGUE

The inner circle gathered together at Welf-Este, a castle overlooking the Danube River in southeastern Bavaria. The Welf dynasty came to power in the middle ages when the Holy Roman Emperor, Frederick the First, awarded Bavaria to the family as fief. They remained in power for the next seven hundred years.

The Illuminati had suffered a setback, but that could be easily fixed. Stanton Price, Jr. had gotten sloppy. The Grand Pindar of the Draco does not involve himself in the messy day to day nuances of Illuminati business. The Grand Pindar is a figurehead. A leader. Perhaps it had been a mistake selecting an American to the post. It would be the topic of discussion. Satanael, the Elder deserved the best that those in the inner circle could muster.

It had already been determined that the President of the United States would be assassinated. Thanks to the extensive work done by the Council of Thirty Three she had been convinced of the need to replace her vice-president. The council made sure she did so with a high ranking Freemason. Everyone has skeletons in their closet. The previous vice-president had hidden the fact he'd once had an illicit encounter with the underage daughter of a member of his staff. That was all it took. Madame President made the switch. She and her new running mate had just won reelection, and done so by an overwhelming majority. The Illuminati was now a heartbeat from sitting in the oval office.

Now to the task at hand. Selecting a new Grand Pindar. He had to be a Druid. Come from the Council of Thirteen. He had to be someone who was prepared to lead the world when the truth was revealed. That day was coming, and coming very soon. Satanael, the Elder would assume his rightful throne and those who dwell on the earth would finally be Illuminated... Or eliminated... Whatever the case may be.

Larry London had caused some trouble no doubt. That had not been foreseen. No one on the council thought the capricious buffoon would become a sniveling born again Christian. Nor did any of them think he would try to seek retribution for a wife and child he never had much to do with anyway. The man's marriage was a joke. He never paid very much attention to his wife, his child, or his marriage. Why he all of a sudden cared was completely lost on them. Not that it mattered. He was sitting in a prison cell in San Quentin doing hard time. By the time he got out the world would be a much different place. He would wish he put that gun to his own head. For all the good he did he might as well have because in the end it didn't matter. Humankind was on a crash course with destiny. Satanael, the Elder would rule over his domain, as he should have been doing from the very beginning.

Throughout history royalty has always crowned their first born. What kind of father would bypass his namesake for an offspring further down the line? Especially the son of an unwed teenage whore. But things would soon be put right. The world had lived in darkness for far too long. The time had come for a new world order. A world Illuminated...

Made in United States
Orlando, FL
30 August 2024